Kosher

by
Kimberly Beam

Behler™
PUBLICATIONS
Behler Publications
California

Behler Publications
California

Kosher
A Behler Publications Book

This is a work of fiction. Names, characters, places, and incidents either are the product of the author's imagination or are used fictitiously. Any resemblance to actual persons, living or dead, events, or locales is entirely coincidental.

Library of Congress Cataloging-in-Publication Data is available
Control Number: 2004108744

FIRST EDITION

ISBN 1-933016-00-0
Published by Behler Publications, LLC
Lake Forest, California
www.behlerpublications.com

Manufactured in the United States of America

To my family:
Mom, Dad, Meredith, Carol, Jonathan and Robin
And to Carolyn,
who helped change my life.

Acknowledgments

Many people have contributed to my life and writing during the time I was writing *Kosher*.

Darcy Steinke guided my first and second scrawlings into something cohesive. Rebecca Brown kicked me in the butt and didn't allow me to slack, as per my request. She also graciously received my frantic call when I thought I lost Alex in my apartment fire.

A special thank you to Kristan Ryan for remembering Alex from when we were at Goddard together. Lynn and Fred Price for giving Alex a home. Karen Novak for her insightful edits. Her guidance takes my writing to a higher level.

Jessica Cushman, life won't be the same with you in Louisville.

Tim, Ann, and Taylor Marton have made me one of their family, letting me write for hours at their kitchen table with a dog on my lap. A special thank you for Saturday night dinners listening to "Says You" on NPR.

Cami Foerster, thank you for your unconditional ear, loving support and for challenging my spiritual life. To her family, Stefan, Darienne and Micah, for feeding me, especially when I forgot to eat. Mimi-mom, my spiritual mom, who prays for me daily, just like one of her kids.

To the Thomas family for opening their home and lives to so many. For the prayer, food and fellowship. To Meg and Amy for being such encouraging readers. To Jim for the photo shoot and being so patient when I got the giggles. To Emily for her friendship. May you all be blessed.

Evalina Harms, who puts up with my clutter and talking to myself when I read aloud. She's taken big risks to do the right thing.

To all my students and youth at youth group. You feed my creativity and keep me laughing.

But most of all to Jesus, my savior, the Father and Holy Spirit. May You be honored in my life and in all I do. All of this is because of You and is completely for You.

Kosher

My sister, Grey, is beautiful. She sparks. Not me. Not Alex Mariner.

Zeke, my older brother, has his blasted jokes and acts like all is a good time. He doesn't do his schoolwork. He plays hockey and drives around fast late at night with his friends, the car windows open, music blaring. I wish I were old enough to drive. Rushing down the road at 90mph, soaring over hills, around turns. Taking the Kamikaze Cliff on two wheels, squealing and screeching around the asphalt, watching solid rock bend out of my way.

I would be King of the world, reining in terror. Instead of being forced to lug around Zeke's massive black hockey equipment bag, I would strap my 75-pound backpack to his left leg and make him lug it around everywhere, even the bathroom. I would make him sit on his face and eat his toes for every time he said I had a smooching lover or picked me up by squeezing my head, calling me, "Stupid" or "Queer" or "Rat" or "Moron." Like he couldn't think up better names?

If I had the power, I would make Zeke talk about himself in third person as Barfing Stooge. "May Barfing Stooge go to the bathroom?" I would make him ask. Of course the answer would be no. "Hold it." Hold it like I have to hold it when he screeches, throwing me over his head and up and down in the air, yelling like the gods above can't hear him. Bellowing over and over, "Jelly Bean, Jelly Bean! We want to see your jelly beans!"

I have no power. I'm Alex. Plain, twelve year old Alex. I'll be the last to be allowed to go away with friends and their parents when they take vacations. No Aruba, Cancun, Ivory Coast for me. I'll be missing out on all of those bronzed women in their stringed bikinis, or no bikinis. Topless women are the bomb, my bomb. The A-bomb that makes me explode mushrooms everywhere.

What am I saying?

When I'm not here, my family doesn't even notice. They

only notice when I'm with Poppy.

Zeke always says when I get back, "Poppy, Poppy will make you sleep...." in the voice of that ugly green witch from *The Wizard of Oz*.

Zeke tries to be in command now. If I don't run the second he barks, I just might get the two liter bottle of Coke over my head to teach me a lesson in prompt obedience.

We all know who's *really* in command.

It's Grey. She speaks and the world listens. She sighs and the world runs to fetch for her. I hate that I'm one of those silly boys too. Grey could ask me to jump off the house just so she could test the density of my bones, and I would do it. Grey, with her short brown curly hair, that all she has to do is run her long fingers through it and every boy would ask her if he could carry her brown papered covered books; buy her lunch outside the cafeteria that always smells of last week's burgers; go to the minimart and pick up sandwiches, run down to Valentino's and get a pizza; give her a ride home in their trucks, cars, whatever they could borrow from their parents just for the occasion; call her for a date on Friday night and take her to a really nice dinner so they could talk. A movie could be good, however, because in a dark scene they would be able to grab her hand, the long skinny hand that had played with her hair and had led them to ask her out in the first place. Not that I would think this way about my sister.

This is what they say in the middle school barely-a-jockstrap locker room. This isn't the only drivel that comes out of a middle school guy's mouth. I guard my ears so I never hear what they say about her in the my-jockstrap-is-bigger-than-your-jockstrap high school locker room.

When I've got the power, there will be no jockstraps. Give everyone an equal playing fear. Hits below the belt will be legal. Suck it up and deal; pain is good for you. Of course, I would never have to play a sport. I would watch the impotent beef-heads, the built up body grunts. They deserve to suffer. I would be better than them. The opposite of now. I would be king, and they would be peons. The athletes would be the lime green scum on the top of the stagnant pond outside the high school that reeks of garbage. The geeks and nerds with their hair sticking up in every direction and brown polyester pants would be gods.

***

Last week one of Zeke's good buddies came up and smacked Poppy on the ass. This kind of idiot stuff is an issue when you have the middle school and high school share hallways, buildings, and locker space. Poppy's locker was open, and she was bending over to put books in her backpack near the end of 4th period study. He came walking by and noticed her cute butt sticking up in the air. Really, who couldn't? She was wearing a short wool skirt and shoes that made her three inches taller. He swung back his massive hand and connected with a solid *smack*. Her voice came out high, like a car siren. She stood up so fast I thought she would topple backwards. She spun around and snapped, "Want to do that again? Right here," and she pointed to her flushed cheek near her mouth.

The guy stammered for a second. He was tall and dumpy. His jeans hung really low and had oil stains on them. His hair was greasy, hanging down around his neck and in his eyes.

"Or maybe you should go back to where you belong," I said. I dumped my books and my Hebrew prayer book went sprawling. Under *normal* circumstances I would have to pick it up and kiss it so as to not offend God. But there was no way in hell I was going to put my two lips on a book in front of anyone I go to school with. I left my books in a heap and stalked down the hallway, toward the oil-stained, brain-dead jerk and Poppy.

"What are you, her girlfriend?" He sneered down at me.

"What's it to you? It's not like you're ever going to get a date with her."

"Why, Jew-boy? You going to stop me?"

I flinched, and my voice came out cold. "No, because she's too good for you."

Matters, our other good friend, was standing nearby at his locker. "Yeah," Matters said, "she's too good for you."

At this, Buddy-of-Zeke's, all greasy and stained, oozed past me, knocking me into the locker, his sneakers scrunching along the fake brick flooring as he reached the place Matters stood. Then he picked Matters up.

"Hey," I said. The guy ignored me. He just starting to squeeze little Matters into the eight inch wide happy yellow locker.

Matters was yelling at the top of his lungs. "Bastard! Bastard, put me down!" He screeched, "Ahhhh!" The guy slammed the locker shut. It sounded like he could be swearing. Once the locker was closed, he sounded like a hamster under a sneaker.

The dork slouched past both Poppy and me as he scrunched his way back over to the high school hallways. We ran to Matters' locker to free him, only he forgot his locker combination. The only set of numbers he could come up with was for locker 1456 at the Y downtown.

"This is not helping," I yelled at him.

"I know," Matters muffled back. "It's the only locker combination I can remember! I've had it since I was five. Of course I'm only going to remember 18-26-36 now." I could hear his voice cracking. Because Matters and I had been friends since kindergarten, I could tell that he was trying hard not to cry.

"I'll go," Poppy said and started to run down the hallway. She turned the corner and I could hear her shoes clapping down the fake brick to the office.

We waited. I kept telling Matters through the metal door that it was all going to be okay. That we would get the combination and he would be out before anyone passed classes.

The clapping shoe sound started again and got closer. Pretty soon, Poppy came flying back around the corner. "Good thing they were swamped and just threw the book at me," she said. She looked at the numbers she had written in sparkly green on the back of her hand and started to turn the black knob with white numbers. She yanked the latch up.

Matters was all smushed into a space his shoulders couldn't exist in, his head bent forward onto his chest. He couldn't squeak out. Seemed as if the brain-dead jerk had super-glued him in there. I tugged at his thin horizontal striped shirt, but Matters didn't budge. Poppy, in her little skirt, squatted down on the floor and pulled at his sneakers, thinking that if those could be free, then the rest would follow out.

A door down the hallway opened and a bunch of kids,

carrying big loads of books started to pour out of the open door.

I had Matters' hand, Poppy his foot and we were pulling on him like mad before any of the battle-ax, uncaring wenches that were our zombie excuses for teachers came out and accused *us* of fun and games and didn't we think it was possible for Matters to get hurt in the locker like that? Hello! Like we would do this to our best friend on purpose. Really woman. Get a life and clothing from this decade.

Poppy and I pulled, and Matters tried to push his way out. We all screamed and tugged, yanked and bellowed, but he was still smushed in there.

What got him out was a miracle and my sister, Grey. She came up and said, "Hey, nice look Matters. Seems like you found the cure for a bad-hair day."

"Ha, Ha, very funny."

"Have you tried laughing your way out?" she asked, turning her head to the side so she could look Matters in the eyes.

"Huh?"

"Yeah," she said. "Laugh."

"At what?" Matters said in irritation. "Really Grey, laugh at what?"

"This. This is funny. You are shoved in a locker and can't get out. Imagine a crowbar having to come, a flare gun, an angry welder with a face mask with *bastard* painted on it."

I chimed in. "Yeah. Captain Underpants, Superman and Wonderwoman all come together to pull on your legs and arms to free you and only Mighty Mouse's 'Here I come to save the day!' is able to do it."

Matters yelled, "Who watches Mighty Mouse?"

"He's cool!" I argued.

"He's old!"

"He's a cartoon. They don't age."

"No, their film breaks and they crumble to pieces." Matters was in no position to be yelling. Grey grabbed his arm from me and winked. I knew how to really get him all pissed so I said, "At least Mighty Mouse is cooler than Bullwinkle. We all know that the Cold War is over and that the Russians are really good people. All Bullwinkle does is add to prejudice."

"Bullwinkle is funny!"

Then, he was off. Matters started frothing and spewing and foaming. He couldn't move, but he was so mad that his body shook in the locker, making the lockers around him rumble. Many people stopped to look; I wanted to charge admission. I wanted to yell, in a freak show announcer voice, "See my best friend, Matters, Ladies and Gentleman! Step right up and see the boy in the box!" Fear of teachers kept me silent.

As Matters barked about Bullwinkle's importance in American culture, Grey took his hand and pulled. He yelled, expanding his lungs and then contracting his lungs which made him even smaller and somehow, all of a sudden, he was out. His mass of brown hair was sticking out, like a miniature afro and his clothing was all crumpled. His shoes looked like they were on crooked, sticking off at wrong angles to his ankles.

Grey's eyes were huge as she stared at him as though she couldn't believe what she just saw. Matters was frowning at everyone still standing around watching. Teachers *still* hadn't noticed.

When at last they did it was only to say, "Come on everyone, let's get to class."

Matters muttered, "I need to go to the bathroom." He took off leaving his bookbag on the floor next to his open locker.

Poppy and I followed him; I lugged his bookbag along. Since it was a rank boy's room, Poppy couldn't follow us in. She was forced to stand outside the heavy wooden door. I was sure she was trying to eavesdrop with her ear to the oak.

Matters was slamming around, kicking stalls, hammering on the paper-towel holder. I was sure Poppy could hear just fine as Matters yelled, "Stupid Idiot! What was he thinking? I'm going to get him. Just wait. I'm going to pummel and nail him so hard that his balls come out of his mouth!"

I wasn't sure how he was going to accomplish that since he was half of the bastard's size. "When I'm king," I said, "you can eat him for dinner."

"Dinner my ass! I'm going to put him on a spit like a stuffed pig, rotate it around a couple of times, smearing bar-b-que sauce all over him and *then* serve him for dinner."

"A cannibal feast? Should we add a gladiator fighting a lion, too?"

"Only if *he's* the one being eaten by the lion," Matters said as he tried to kick the paper towel holder, which was way too high up on the wall to even come near his foot. He just swung his leg wildly in the area of the light blue wall. After he missed, he bellowed and punched the holder instead.

"Effective," I said. "Are you ready to go now?" I was worried teachers would hear him and come in to see what was going on. We were already late for class and that meant I would probably get detention.

***

When I came home from camp this summer, I told Matters that I had met the most amazing kisser. He asked how I knew she was so amazing since she was the only girl I had ever kissed. I said, "Her lips had uncontrollable power."

I said, "Her name was Shellia. She's amazing in the water. You should see what she could do."

Shellia was at summer camp. She was in the oldest girl's dorm: Building E. I would watch her as she would sneak out at night. Only it wasn't me who got to experience her. I felt kind of bad lying to Matters, but I wanted to be cool. I wanted to do stuff no one else had, have power and gain popularity. I wanted to be King of the middle school.

Too bad one of the guys had sex this summer, huh? Unless he was like me and lied through his metal-mouth.

He was King though, and you had to respect monarchy.

***

Zeke had me over his head again. Picked me up in the family room and said that he was going to powerhouse me into the carpet. He held my entire body over his head, one arm had my legs and the other my chest. I screamed like hell to be put down.

He started jumping up and down, this time yelling: "Rodents, Rodents, you've got a hamster in your pants! I want to see your hamsters! I want to see your hamsters!"

Grey was nowhere to be seen. Not that she would have

protected me if she were there.

Zeke thought this was funny.

If I could have, I would show him funny. I would show him the hamster he says I've got in my pants. I would let it flop around for him to see. I would spew yellow rivers at him. I would put hamsters in his underwear when he was sleeping and drooling on his rancid pillow. Let's see what kind of dreams that gave him.

It was no wonder I slept with my door locked at night. If I grew up to be some serial killer or the Unibomber or something they could just point to the abuse my older brother inflicted. Of course, I shouldn't let all of this distract me whenever I'm home, in the family room watching T.V. hoping that Zeke didn't come in and start his little games.

After all, Zeke was just Barfing Stooge.

***

I was in the study in the back of house, where Mom and Dad hide to think. There were two desks in there and two large armchairs. One high backed and with kind of hard cushions. The other was low back. When you sunk into it, every desire to be anywhere else left. Even if I had to pee, I would hold it for hours just because I didn't want to leave the soft, swallowing chair.

Zeke was watching Beevis and Butthead reruns and was thinking about turning me into Lake Titikaka. I had out my prayer book and Torah portion to study for my Bar Mitzvah, the day I would be a man in the eyes of everyone Jewish. I still couldn't drive a car. I was still at the mercy of my mom and Grey because wherever they wanted to go, we went. Art museums, coffee shops and freak clothing stores where we're forced to watch her try to find a reason to buy crinoline. Who cares what a girl wears under her skirt, it's what's under the crinoline that matters.

Grey came into the doorway. She was tall and a junior in high school.

"Hey," she said.

"Hi."

"You hiding?" She came in and shut the door. I was in the

good chair, the swallowing one, and she took the other, Dad's.

"I'm concerned about you," she said sitting straight backed, the only way the chair allowed you to sit.

"Why?"

"Zeke."

"Yeah, well. You got to take what you got to take."

"He doesn't abuse me like he does you," Grey said. She chucked her head to the side to indicate Zeke in the family room. "So what are you going to do about it?"

"I've got big plans," I said, "for when I become King."

"And in the meantime?"

"Hide."

***

At dinner that night, Mom and Dad looked at each other.

"So, Zeke, you figured out where you're going to apply to college yet?" said Dad.

Oh, dear, the college discussion. Dinner conversation had turned down this road many times before and it never ended well. Zeke was a senior and should have had all of this done already. I already knew that Grey was on top of all of this and had at least a six-inch stack of prospective college information. Grey calls it propaganda; Zeke calls it a hassle; I think it's really cool to look at.

"Could I please have the steak?" I said.

"I'd rather not talk about it," Zeke mumbled as he pushed his corn around his plate.

"Could I please have the steak?" I pointed toward the platter.

Grey reached way over across the table in front of Zeke and handed the platter to me.

"Thanks," I said.

"I think this is a good time to talk about it, Zeke." Dad put down his fork. "You need direction and it's not found on the football field or out with friends."

Zeke was just trying to get Dad off his back. We'd all seen his tactics before.

"Have you been to your guidance counselor?" Mom said.

"I'm sure Mrs. Miglochney will have information for you."

Zeke's face started to turn red but he still refused to look up.

"Now, financial aid is going to be an issue. If you don't pick a school, then well, you might not be able to go because of money," Mom continued.

"Listen," Grey said as she stared down Zeke. I looked at her shocked. We never get involved in parental discussions about one another. It was like this understood thing.

Grey continued, "You don't have to apply to Yale or Harvard and be like our cousin Marc. You just need to go to a school you're happy with."

Dad looked at her. "Have *you* seen Mrs. Miglochney?"

"Yup," she said and stuck some red skinned potatoes in her mouth so she couldn't say anything more.

"And...?" Dad wasn't about to let her off the hook.

"I've got some schools I would really like to see."

"We should talk more," he said.

"I would like that." She smiled.

Dad sighed and turned back to Zeke. "On Wednesday of next week, you and I are sitting down and we're going to go through what you've come up with. I want a plan for the next six months in regards to schools and financial aid. I also want to see at least five schools you are seriously considering. If you don't meet with me, Zeke, your mother and I will meet to discuss *our* plans for you next year. Is that understood?"

Zeke looked at Dad and then at Mom and said, "May I be excused? I don't want dessert. I have a date."

***

I was skulking around the corner, hiding in the bushes, creeping up to the corner of the house. Zeke had taken out the most beautiful girl in school. She was the field hockey captain and had long blonde hair. Her blue eyes sparkled like the ocean on a clear day and her body was all muscle that quivered when she moved. She was a cheetah whose presence in the hallways at school made everyone stare. And lucky for me, Zeke had brought her back to the house.

I heard him say, "Want to take a walk?"

"Where?" She sounded suspicious.

With one eye peeking around the corner and through the bushes, I saw him say, "The woods."

She looked around for a moment. "Maybe," she said. "What are we going to do there?"

"Oh, walk around, you know."

"I don't know....I don't think so."

"Come on," he said. "It will be good fun."

The smell of pine was strong. The bush in front of me was pricking my arms through my long-sleeved T-shirt. I was wearing a fleece vest which was helping to keep me warm. My hands were cold and needed some prompting to follow my brain's orders. The garden hose with the yellow spray gun was set for stun, armed and ready. My hands were doing as I wanted despite the cold water running down them making my whole body shiver and shake.

The field hockey captain wasn't saying anything. Zeke continued his sales pitch, "You know. I'll treat you real nice, and you can say whatever you want. We can look up at the stars and you can tell me all you know about astrology."

I shook my head at his ignorance.

"Astronomy," she corrected.

"Right, that's what I said. Astronomy. ...You could tell me the names of the trees and I could tell you if you're right or not." It sounded pretty lame to me. No wonder the girl was hesitant to go. *Hamsters, my ass.* I took aim.

Zeke started to talk to her about other stuff and put his arm out to her face. I could see better by bobbing my head through the bushes. She pulled away a little and I heard her say, "Perhaps you should take me home."

I hollered at them, "Sounds like a GREAT idea!"

"What the hell?" I heard Zeke say. But then the sound of water drowned out everything else he might have added. At first I stayed hidden in the bushes like a guerrilla. Then I burst out in the open and dowsed him with cold water that this November night made freeze.

I faced him head on.

I hit below the belt, for this is legal. I let the peon have it, like he made me have it.

The girl, poor thing, screamed and put her hands up to her mouth, eyes wide in terror. Zeke was ready to pummel me, squash me into the mud that I had created with the hose.

"Come here!" He grabbed for me blinded by icy water. "Come here and face me like a man!"

"Treat me like a man and I will face you like one!"

"Give me that hose!" He leapt grabbing at the air for the hose that I still had on full blast, pointing at his crotch and any other body part that he might have put in the way of a direct hit, his hand, his head, his legs, whatever. Within moments, he was drenched, like a weasel held underwater.

The girl was no longer screaming. She was watching with a wide grin on her face.

"Sorry if I get you wet," I yelled to her as I continued to blast Zeke.

Zeke was swearing like he swears when Mom and Dad aren't home. Only they were home and standing on the porch next to the girl who was grinning; she seemed to be enjoying this as much as I was. Mom and Dad frowned, but at whom, I couldn't tell. I was too busy making sure Zeke couldn't get me.

He started to put his hand out to the stream, all hunched over, walking toward me. "Pussy boy, you are going to pay!"

"You are paying right now. I'm getting you back for every hamster, jelly bean and rodent you've put me through!"

Mom was furious. "Zeke! Watch your mouth!"

Dad said, "Okay, boys. I want you to stop right now."

"Watch me stop him!" Zeke lowered his head and rushed me.

I locked the hose on high spray and dropped it, so that it danced all over the yard, spraying water in erratic fountains between Zeke and me. I took off like the Grim Reaper was after me with his scythe ready to lop off my head. My feet moved. My body pushed and I headed directly for the woods that Zeke wanted to take the girl to. I crashed into the crunching leaves and grabbing branches. I lost myself in the trees. I didn't look behind me until I was deep in the underbrush and swallowed by the pines. I knew these woods so well it didn't matter if it was dark or not. I knew where I was headed and it wasn't home.

***

I skulked up the grass beside Poppy's gravel driveway. Walking on the gravel would have been too loud. Her parents might have heard. I was only supposed to visit during set times, and 11:00 p.m. on a Friday night was not on their schedule.

When I showed up at her closed window and knocked, she jumped about two inches off her still unmade bed and screamed like she did in the hallway when that guy slapped her. She smiled at herself as she slid off the mattress and silently heaved the window open for me. The light next to her bed was on, giving off a pale yellow glow that I had followed from around the front of the house. We sat on her floor after she had turned on a CD of classical music, cranking the volume up loud. Her parents didn't mind loud music so long as it was classical.

Her parents were down in her family room, in the finished basement, watching a movie.

I stayed long enough to know that I wouldn't get in too much trouble from Zeke when I walked in. I was hoping that if I left Poppy's house at 12:30, I would get home at 1:00 and then there was a very high likelihood that my parents would already be in bed.

I'm not that lucky. I walked up the drive and went to the sliding doors on the porch off the family room. The lights in the kitchen were on. Mom and Dad were still up. A blue flickering glow from the family room also let me know that Zeke was watching T.V. Grey was probably out with friends. I knew I was toast.

I slid open the glass door in the family room. Zeke didn't notice, even though I was practically right next to him. I tiptoed past him and hoped to all heaven I wasn't leaving footprints on the carpet. Dousing your brother with the hose and running away was bad enough, leaving mud on the carpet was a crime worthy of grounding in my house. I looked back and in the blue glow from the T.V., I could see my life was about to be over.

I tried to sneak past the kitchen door, but Dad called out to me, "Hey, Sport, you want some ice cream?"

Ice cream? My hands were stiff and my feet were so cold I wasn't sure I could feel them any longer. I had shivered in

Poppy's bedroom and she had given me a fleece blanket that she had on the back of her reading chair. She'd had me take off my shoes and socks and put my feet on the heater. That felt good, but I had to put the wet stuff back on to get home. I was still shivering.

I stuck my head into the kitchen. "You know, Dad," I said with a grin through my chattering teeth, "I think I'm a little too cold for ice cream." My shivering hand tapped the white painted door frame.

"Go put on your PJ's and some wool socks and come on down for some hot cocoa."

"I would much rather just go on up to bed."

"This isn't a debate," he said. "Be down in five minutes."

Mom was at the breakfast bar, staring at me as I turned and went up to change.

I came back down wearing a navy blue sweatshirt that used to be Dad's and a pair of blue, black and gray plaid flannel pants. Mom was watching Dad pour water into the rounded white ceramic mugs. I sat down at the breakfast bar next to her, facing Dad, who was mixing the cocoa at the stove. He handed both mugs up to Mom and me. "So, Sport, want to tell us what's been going on?"

"Do I have a choice?"

Dad shook his head. I looked at Mom. She was looking at me with her eyebrows raised; her eyes fixed on mine. Mom didn't often talk; she didn't need to. Her silences spoke more than most people's words.

"It's nothing," I said.

"That didn't look like nothing," Dad said.

"Zeke did say he has been giving you a real hard time," Mom said softly.

"So?"

"So, you blasted Zeke with a hose on his big date," Dad said. "He drove the girl home and shivered all the way there and back. When he got back, his lips were blue."

"Why didn't he change his clothes first?"

"He did."

"Oh." I stared at the light brown cocoa foam inside my mug.

"I want to know something," Mom said.

Dad and I both looked at her.

"What's a hamster?"

"It's a small, furry nocturnal animal," I said completely serious.

"That's not what you meant with Zeke."

"I would rather not talk about it."

Dad sighed. "Alex, your mother and I need to come up with an appropriate punishment for both of you. If we don't have all the information, we cannot be fair."

"Do what you think is right. Can I go? I'm really tired."

"Are you going to tell us where you were?"

"The woods."

"We thought you may have gone to Matters'," Dad said.

"Nope. I wasn't there."

"What about Poppy's?" Mom's voice was still soft.

"Can I go to bed now?"

"Let us sleep on this, and tomorrow morning we will tell you what we think."

I slid off the stool and left a mostly full mug of hot cocoa on the counter to get cold.

***

At school on Monday they were all talking about it. It got around that Alex Mariner had ruined Zeke Mariner's date with the hottest girl in school by turning the hose on him. I became popular for a day. Everybody was smacking me on the back and telling me what a good job it was. "What a fantastic prank; wish I could have done it myself."

The village idiot of my year said, "Really Alex, didn't know you had it in you."

I wanted to hide. The truth of the matter was, Zeke and I had both gotten in trouble. I was grounded; big whoop, like I had anywhere to go. They put a restraining order on a guy I live with. Zeke, or any projectile that came from him, was not allowed within a five-foot radius of me. We all knew that restraining orders are made to be broken.

Mom had known a woman at work. This woman, who was

also a nurse, was having troubles with her boyfriend and got a restraining order put on him. The weekend after she got it in place, he murdered her. Mom had come home crying and wasn't herself for two weeks.

I was waiting for Zeke to violate his. Just like that boyfriend. Zeke had taken to chucking everything at me, including cups full of juice and water, and they were all aimed for the five feet around me. When the juice would splatter all over the white linoleum kitchen floor, he would bark, "Clean that up, you slob," and walk away.

Not all of the cups of stuff landed outside the five feet. I needed to change my pants about once a day. In the afternoons, while making sandwiches or getting a granola bar out of the pantry, a cup of juice or water would come flying at my butt, or hip or crotch.

After the liquid seeped in a little, I would look up at him, blank faced and say nothing. I would take my food and go find clean clothes. I knew Mom would begin to figure it out, like when she had to start getting red juice dye out of the seat of my pants.

Zeke would chuckle and say, "You wait boy. What you have waiting for you is worse than jelly beans and hamsters. You wait."

"That's right," I said. "You threaten me and I'll get the restraining order renewed."

The truth was, whenever I saw him, I shook all over. My teeth chattered and I was just waiting for him to strike out, land on me and suffocate me to death.

The girl he had been on the date with wouldn't talk to him anymore. Instead, she talked to me. When I passed her in the hallways she called out, "Little Mariner!"

I turned, only to be blinded each time by her blond hair and tight sweaters. She'd say, "How you doing?"

"Good," I would stammer, trying really hard not to stare at her huge chest.

"Where you going?"

"Class."

"Can I walk you?" So the cheetah, whose name was Michelle, would walk me to class.

I was a seventh grader being walked to class by a senior in high school. She thought of me like a little brother. She called me, "Kid" and "Cutie" and she even tousled my hair. You didn't tousle the hair of someone you were attracted to. You did it to your little brother to tick him off.

Of course I grinned at her like some stupid smiley face and prayed to God that she didn't notice that I was standing up to attention, saluting her with everything I had.

***

Matters was jealous. "You get all the cute girls," he said.

"Where?" I looked around trying to find them.

"Poppy and now this Michelle; And there's always Shellia from summer camp."

"Right," I said. "Poppy has never been and is never going to be mine. Michelle thinks of me as a cute kid that she finds amusing. And Shellia has forgotten all about me; I haven't heard from her in ages. This is stupid. Why are we talking about this?"

Matters didn't answer. He was staring at the clump of trees by the golf course about four blocks from my house.

"What?"

"Zeke's up there," he said.

"Right," I said and turned my course towards Poppy's. "Looks like we'll need to take a detour."

"Don't you think this is fun?"

I said nothing.

"Do you think Poppy will mind us dropping in on her like this?"

"I really don't care. Zeke wants to kill me and I think I want him to do it soon, because I don't know how much longer I can live like this."

***

Grey came to her window when I knocked on it. She shoved it open.

"You should have heard him when he came in. All bitter

because you had dodged his plans. He had sticks to pummel you with and pinecones to shove down your pants."

"Great," I said as I crawled in. "I don't know how much more I can take. Part of me wants to turn myself over and take whatever he wants to give me. It has to better than living this way."

"He's in the family room, if you want." Of course he would stop if Grey told him to. She could get the world to stop rotating on its axis if she asked it.

"I'm going to go in there and take it like a man, even though he thinks I'm a boy."

"Alex," she said, "you don't have to do this. Just tell moma and dad what he's been doing. They will remove your punishment and give him a much stricter one."

"Yeah, then I would be bombarded with flying water balloons in my bed. No thank you."

***

At first Zeke didn't want to accept my surrender. But I called him chicken and stupid, and impotent, and flaccid-king. He got up and got his revenge. It was over. I showered away the whipped cream down the front of my pants. I scrubbed the raspberry jelly out of my hair. He kept it clean, relatively. Of course he did give me a massive wedgie in the process. We won't go into how high up it went, what got jammed around or how long he held me in the air by my underwear. All I would say was that Zeke was now satisfied, he had gotten his revenge and all was squared up.

It was a good thing Zeke was stupid. See, he would go into school and tell the story, but it was just a story. What I did was seen by field hockey captain, Michelle. What I did was save me a whole bunch of humiliation. All I had to do was roll my eyes and say, "Don't believe everything you hear," and everybody would start questioning what really happened. My pride and face were saved and Zeke still didn't look so good. I'd won both ways. Of course, I wasn't able to sit down the next day. I considered going commando, sans underwear, out of fear of boxers even hurting. Anyway, I was better than Zeke and that made me great.

***

Poppy said, "Hey, Alex."

I turned. Her dark brown, massive curls exploded out of her ponytail, her legs were long, her body full. I pulled my eyes back to my locker.

"What's up?" I was unable to keep my eyes away from her.

"Oh, nothing," she said leaning against the wall next to me. Her chest was round and full and my hands wanted to find out if they felt like water balloons.... Her books were pressed against them. She didn't notice my staring; she was watching the masses pass.

"You need to cover that... math book," I blurted just in case she did see me staring. "Mrs. Alberta may hurt you."

"Yeah, I know. You got anything in there that could help?"

She turned to look in my locker. My jacket hung on that little hook thing on the side and my books were shoved in a big heap at the bottom. "What about up top?" she asked as she pushed the lever on the side of the locker up. The very top one popped open. She looked up, her deep blue eyes caressed the locker fathoms away.

She grinned, looking me up and down. She was standing four inches taller than me because of the clunky heels on her black shoes. "I guess you don't use it much, huh?"

I grunted. She giggled. A sweet throaty almost hiccup of a laugh that rang in my head for the rest of the morning.

***

Grand Marnier. That's what my father was drinking out of a short bubbled glass as he stood over the fireplace three nights later, a Friday night to be exact. We'd just gotten home from Friday night services, where attendance was a requirement if I was to have my Bar Mitzvah as planned in March. I don't even want to start on that one.

I had no other plans. Not that I could have plans. I was still grounded.

"So, Alex," Dad said. "I see you haven't been hiding around the house like you were at the beginning of the week. Why aren't you afraid of Zeke anymore?"

I said nothing and stared at the burning logs, yellow-orange and blue, in the fire.

"Well?" I could feel him looking at me from the mantle. If I could have gotten my tongue to form words in my mouth, I would have said, "I'm in love with whipped cream. Zeke is a pervert. The second I think of what happened my toes turn scarlet and my mouth becomes covered over with flesh. The flesh forms a seal never to be broken, never to utter another syllable. I will deny what he did, even to myself."

I just raised an eyebrow to my father.

He raised his back, "It must have been messy."

I stared.

"Do I need to know?"

"Do I need to tell?"

His green eyes locked on mine and he started to bore it out. His eyes penetrated mine so that the room got even hotter. I could feel my shirt beginning to stick to me as my armpits began to flow, and I sank into the couch. I could feel my pulse racing in my neck. I could hear its pounding in my ears, "TELL. JUST TELL!"

But then he turned his back on me and stared into the fire. Cool relief coursed through my veins.

***

Tuesday afternoons I was forced to have Bar Mitzvah tutoring with the Rabbi's wife.

"Now pronounce this after me," the Rabbi's wife said as her lips curved around foreign words, foreign letters that made no sense.

I tried.

"No," she said. "There isn't a vowel there. You need to flow it together more. And it's not AY, it's AH."

"Right," I said, still not understanding.

She had to be around 45, black haired with gray sprinkled

throughout. It was longish, straight and down to her shoulders.

And, she was married to the rabbi.

I was in the rabbi's house. At the rabbi's kitchen table, where the rabbi ate breakfast every morning. As I looked across to the other end of the white Formica table with a wicker basket of oranges in the center, I could picture the rabbi, his dark hair sticking up all over and in his long sleeved, blue-with-little-pinstripe pajamas sitting down to eat Shredded Wheat.

"Ah-doe-nie-ech-ahd. Bar-uch shame kil-vode mal-chu-toe..." I said.

She cut me off, frowning, "You've known the Shema since you were in the second grade. Read what's in front of you."

"I didn't practice," I admitted with my eyes glued to the paper in front of me.

"Again?" she asked.

I didn't say anything. The white of the table was blinding. I couldn't read the black squiggles of Hebrew in front of me. She sighed and sat back in her chair. She exuded a sense of properness. And I didn't live up to her expectations.

"Next week," she said, "if you haven't attended synagogue and you haven't studied, we will not be meeting."

"Okay."

"Now, let's go over what you need to do this week." She opened my prayer book and started to walk me through sections I would be reading out loud to the congregation.

***

At the end of the session, when she finally let me go, I walked out the front door, my bookbag slung over one of my shoulders. I looked at my watch. Zeke was ten minutes late to pick me up. I waited another five and realized he wasn't coming at all.

I threw the other arm of my backpack over my other shoulder, slunked down the driveway and started a bitter cold walk home. My feet moved forward; my shoulders began to scream with pain. I kept up a fast pace because the sun was setting, and I wanted to get home before dark. It was blocks and blocks. As I was passing the Hess station, I thought about stopping and getting some Twinkies, but then realized that I had to keep moving if I was going to get home before my parents. The trees were already dark fingers scratching the golden sky.

When I got to my street, I chanted over and over in my head, 'Almost there. Almost there,' like that guy in Star Wars whose mission was to blow up the Death Star and instead gets himself blown up.

When I came in the front door, Zeke was in front of the T.V. eating Doritos. I sneaked past him, trying really hard to control my mouth and arms from attacking him. I went and hid in the study.

***

Mom started out the dinner conversation that night, "Got a call from the rabbi's wife today."

"What she want?" Zeke said with a mouth full of food.

"You could pay attention more to those around you," Dad said in quiet disapproval. "She's tutoring Alex for his Bar Mitzvah."

"Oh, right. Bar Mitzvah. Ha-Ha. Like he'll ever be an adult," Zeke said, chewing. "He's still got a security blanket, Yaba. Yaba." He continued to repeat my security blanket's name over and over again.

"We're more concerned about your ever being an adult," Dad's disapproving tone was clearer.

Grey almost snarfed. "Dad just insulted you, Zeke."

"Dad, your parents still wonder about you," Zeke said in a lame comeback.

"Not good enough," Grey said as she added more cranberry sauce to her plate. "Try something better."

Zeke sat and thought while playing with the food on his plate.

"Don't strain yourself too much," Grey continued. "You might burst a blood vessel in your brain and give yourself a stroke."

"An aneurysm," I corrected.

"Whichever will hurt more."

"Saw you in Grunge-Boy's Jeep today," Zeke fired at Grey

across the table.

Mom and Dad, at either end, turned to her.

"What about it?" She chewed on her chicken.

"Grunge-Boy?" Mom's eyebrows were raised.

"His real name is Merriman," Grey said. "He's a nice guy."

"He's got a nice Jeep," I said. "It's one of the cooler cars in the parking lot."

Nobody was really listening to me, so I continued, "Much cooler than Zeke's bomb."

A glare from Zeke. "Hey!" He pointed his fork at me. "Only I am able to-" he pointed his fork to his chest and then back at me "-talk that way about that car. If you want rides in it, you need to treat it with respect."

"Does that mean you are going to start giving me rides?" I asked.

"You don't give him rides?" Dad said.

"I, um, sure, I give him rides all the time, right Alex?"

I looked at him, but said nothing.

Mom set her next bite back on the plate. "How did you get home today, Alex? Zeke was supposed to bring you home after your tutoring."

"I walked."

Mom turned to Zeke. "How could you?" She practically spit. "You let him walk home three and a half miles?"

"Come on, Mom," Zeke said playing with his food. He could barely meet her gaze. "It's not like he got hurt or anything and he got home before you did."

"I am so pissed at you, I could throw you out of this house," Mom hissed.

We all stared at her shocked. Mom never spoke like this.

Dad sighed. "Maybe we should take some time and cool down before we discuss this."

"Maybe we should take away his car," Mom said.

"A good thought," Dad said. "Let's talk about it after dinner and enjoy the rest of our meal."

Zeke was in hot water, and more important, Grey's ride in Merriman's cool Jeep was forgotten. She looked at me across the table and winked her thanks. I asked for more peas.

***

The next day Poppy and I were sitting in the forced silence of the school's media center (it's *not* a library - though it looks an awful lot like one and anyone from the normal world would call it that). I asked her, "What kind of name is Merriman?"

"Well." She chewed on her pen cap. Her insane curls were invading her face. She had put on a little make-up, which she almost never did. Her eyes were bright and sparkling, like the lake I learned to water-ski on, like the ocean under a noon sun.

"It comes from...," she chewed a bit longer. "Okay, in a book series I read once, it was the name of Merlin. It was his modern name: Merriman."

"Merlin, as in King Arthur?" I was a little surprised.

"Yeah, you know, knights of the round table," She burst into whispered song, a jumpy, lilting, happy song that came from a movie we had watched together on a Saturday night a couple of months back. We'd had the lights turned off and the popcorn bowl between us. I thought more about her body next to mine and how warm she made me than I thought about the movie. Once our hands met in the greasy popcorn bowl and lingered for a few sweaty moments, but she pulled hers out. I followed.

"Why do you want to know?" She snapped the gnawed cap back over the tip of the pen.

"Oh," I said, my eyes locked on those tiny wet bite marks as I tried to remember what we were talking about. Oh yeah, Merriman. "He took Grey out yesterday after school and I was just wondering about his name. Names tend to mean a lot about a person."

"Merriman Winters. He's so hot."

"What?"

"That guy could have anyone he wants. Well, he could have me. I wouldn't mind at all."

"His nickname is Grunge-Boy."

"Isn't that so cool? He skips school on Fridays to go snowboarding. I hear he's in these big time competitions *and* he wears the Abercrombie and Fitch cologne. He's just amazing."

"For a second there, you actually sounded like a girl," I said staring at her.

Poppy sat back with a small pout on her face. "Maybe if you took a little notice, I *am* a girl."

"No you're not. You're much cooler."

She started to collect her books. "Really Alex. I thought we were friends." She bit down on the pen again.

"We are." I said, as I watched her collect her stuff.

She was so vehement with what she was doing that as she reached for the book near me, her arm swiped the pen in her mouth and flung it across the table, spraying spit as it flew.

"I'm not so sure," she said as she stood up, not even noticing the stream of saliva on the table.

"We're in a library," I pointed out to her.

"It's a *media center*. And you'll get a lot more done without my bothering you," she said as she turned and walked away.

I don't get it. I haven't a clue what I said. It's like all of a sudden she totally wigged out. Maybe she's getting her period, ewww, or something. I almost gagged and then opened my book.

***

The next day was Wednesday and since Poppy and I still weren't talking, I was forced to keep company with Matters. As we walked down the hallway to lunch, he asked, "How do you keep it all straight?"

"What?" I said.

"All you do. Studying for your Bar Mitzvah, tutoring for math...."

Before I could answer he asked, "When are you going to start talking to Poppy again?"

"Whenever she gets over her red tide. Really, that girl!"

Matters rolled his eyes at me. "If I was a bigger man, I would check you into that locker."

"But you're not, so I'll squeeze you into it instead."

He frowned, glared at me and then looked down.

"Hey, Little Mariner, where you headed?"

Only one person called me Little Mariner. It was Michelle, the Cheetah. She was walking right toward me.

Zeke was right behind her.

He had lost his car indefinitely and there was even talk of

giving it to Grey when she got her license in a couple of months. He was seething mad at me; I could tell he wanted my blood.

I felt my cheeks get warm and the fountains in my armpits began to spray. "Lunch," I said to Michelle, trying to sound real cool and put together.

"Care if I join you?" She turned to walk with me, so we were both walking toward Zeke, who was approaching like death.

I shook my head but dared not speak. Zeke's eyes locked onto mine.

The Cheetah put her arm around my shoulders. I wished she would bring her hand up and start playing with my hair. Zeke passed on my right, he leaned in and softly said in my ear as we cruised by each other, "Watch this." A couple of steps beyond me, Zeke yelled, "Hey, Michelle!"

She stopped and turned to him, dropping her arm from my shoulders in the process. I wanted to grab her hand and put it back. It took almost all of my strength to stop myself.

"I heard Alex talking in his sleep last night. It sounded like a wet-dream about you."

It got dead silent in the hallway.

I felt myself turn even brighter red and wished to God above, if He even existed, that the gray and blue checkered flooring would separate and take me under. Even if it was the pit of hell, all red, fiery. Even if it blistered my skin to complete puss. It would have to be better than this.

Then, all of a sudden, my brain clicked in gear and I heard myself say: "Zeke, you wouldn't know a wet-dream if it landed its spoogy self on your leg. I heard you admit to your best-friend, Goss, just last week that you've never had one."

Zeke turned a red that I was sure matched my own. Michelle laughed, which gave me courage.

"I consider it an honor that Michelle makes it into my dreams, too bad she never gets there for you."

The crowd that we had drawn in the hallway sniggered. They were standing all around us, so that the space between Zeke and me was open. Zeke's shadow in the flooring was distorted and taller than he was, making him seem monstrous and ready to pounce. He could hurt me right here and glancing around, there was nowhere to run. Bright blue lockers were on either side, a couple of classroom doorways, but no place of protection.

Zeke opened his mouth but nothing came out.

Michelle tugged on my arm and continued our walk to lunch.

"Is it true?" she whispered as the crowd opened to allow us to pass through.

"Which? That he heard me or that I've dreamt about you?"

"Either."

I had no clue what she looked like at that moment. Overpowering heat consumed my head and overtook my ears, making them flare. I couldn't answer. If I said no, then she would feel, like, put down or something. If I said yes, then I was a pervert. There wasn't any way to respond. I was stuck. No light. No air. Nothing to say.

She laughed. It rung in my head like a cool shower after a run.

"Not a fair question, huh?" she asked.

I shook my head.

"Well, tell me this," she said. "Has Zeke ever dreamt about me?"

"I have no idea," I said. "You'll have to ask him."

"Or Goss," she replied.

"Or Goss."

***

That night was Wednesday night and as Dad promised he called Zeke into the family room. "Bring all your stuff," he said.

I zoomed out of there as fast as I could.

"Not going to stick around, Sport?" Dad asked me as I was in the doorway.

"No way," I replied turning to him. "It could be World War III in here, and I want no part of it."

Dad chuckled. "I wish I could flee too, but it looks like we might have to go a couple of rounds first."

Zeke walked in. He had a binder with him and a couple of packets from colleges were in his hand, but it didn't look like much.

"Good luck," I mumbled as I left.

If Dad wasn't in the room, I know he would have pushed me over or kicked me or something. But, because Dad was there, he just ignored me.

***

It was a total of four days and Poppy and I still weren't talking. The longest we had gone without speaking to each other was five days and I didn't want it to go that long. Besides, I had a burning question to ask her.

"So, what's he like?" I asked as I came up behind Poppy in the hallway.

"What's who like?" Ice cubes practically dropped from her lips she was so cold.

"Merriman," I said like I didn't even notice she was still mad.

"I wouldn't know, I've never talked to him. If you're so interested, you should ask Grey. She's the one who went for a ride in his Jeep."

I paused for a minute, confused. "Oh, no. I meant Merriman in the books you read."

"Indescribable," she said with a toss of her hair as she turned away.

"Was he evil?" I asked following her.

"No, he was good. Look, if you're so interested, the books are by Susan Cooper. *The Dark is Rising* series. Read them yourself."

"Do you have them?"

Poppy started to walk faster.

I had to jog to keep up with her. "Look, can I borrow them from you?" I asked between gasping breaths.

She stopped dead in the hallway and didn't even slide. She was so graceful it amazed me. I, on the other hand, came close to face-planting and slid about halfway down the hall. Before I could recover, she was frothing.

"Stop, Alex," she said. "Really. Just apologize for being a complete ass and stop pretending to be interested in something you obviously aren't just so you have a reason to talk to me."

"I was not a complete ass! You were the one who got all touchy and defensive.... You were the one who huffed off."

She rolled her eyes. "You don't get it, do you?"

"Get what?"

"Like I said, 'ass'," and she pivoted to walk past me in the other direction. I had to restart my jog to keep up with her and before I knew it, she turned into her French class by making a fast left. For a couple of seconds, I didn't notice that I was scuffing down the hallway alone.

***

Later that day in the Media Center, I had walked down random aisles, pulled books off the shelves and arranged them all over the table around me. Astronomy was to my right and Ancient Egypt was to my left. Hey, if I needed to, I could say that they were part of this total kick-butt interdisciplinary research paper. What *Horticulture and You* was doing there, I wasn't quite sure. Not that I knew exactly what horticulture was, but the picture of an English garden on the front was pretty cool.

I was nearly wetting my pants for wanting Poppy to come in and see me so bad. I wanted her to see that I could be absorbed in important stuff and not need her. I could take care of myself, look I found all these books on my own. She wasn't the only brain around here. I felt someone coming toward the table; I kept my head down.

"Hear you been asking about me."

I looked up. Merriman was standing there, his blond hair was a bit long and kind of shagged in his eyes. He had on a green and white plaid flannel shirt with a white T-shirt underneath that had something written on it that I couldn't read. When he smiled, two large crater dimples appeared in his cheeks and the sides of his eyes got all squinty. He pulled up a chair and began thumbing through *Marine Biology*.

"Huh?" I said not even hearing what he had said.

"Normally I wouldn't care about what some seventh grader thinks of me," he continued like I had any idea why he was there. "But you are Grey's brother and hold a bit of a reputation."

"You're friends with my sister?" I said, still not catching on. Guys who liked Grey never spoke to me. I was too low down in the food chain to matter to them. Besides, I was in the middle school's *media center*. High schoolers are never caught dead in here, unless they're the desperate boys getting excited over the *National Geographics*.

"You're a smart kid," he said.

How would he know?

"Try not to show it all the time."

I looked away. This was too weird.

"Those fights with Zeke and walks to class with Michelle get you noticed."

That was enough. I had to know. "Do you want to kick my ass, or something?"

Merriman laughed. "No."

"Then why are you here?" I said leaning forward.

"Want to go out to Starbucks after school?"

I looked at him in disbelief. "Why?"

"Like I said, I heard you were asking about me."

"Will Grey be there?"

"She could be, but...." He leaned forward and stared me hard in the face. "I'm going to play it straight with you. You sort of need a positive older brother in your life. Your real brother isn't exactly the pinnacle of intelligence. I hate seeing you put on display to try to save your skin all the time."

"Look," I said, about to get up.

"Shh," he whispered looking around for the librarian. "You can swing real good. You've got bite, but life doesn't have to be that hard. You know? You can chill, have fun and not have to worry about who's going to hurt you next."

I laughed to cover up the lump rising in my throat. Who was this freak with his hair all shaggy in his eyes. What does he *really* know about me?

"So I'll see you at my Jeep after school?"

"Sure." I couldn't help it; it just came out.

"Good," Merriman hit the table with his left hand, stood up and walked away.

Afterwards I considered standing him up. But that little

speech of his....

***

At Starbucks, Merriman told me to snag the big brown swallowing armchairs up by the front window while he went to order. When I asked him what he was getting me, he said to trust him. There's a scary thought. The ride over was pretty cool; he played funky music that you could feel in the seats.

When I went over toward the big windows and sat down, the chair was even more comfortable than the one in the study. Merriman came back; he handed me a white cardboard cup with a white plastic cover and a cardboard sleeve. When I pulled the sleeve down a little, there was a black woman in a circle with weird wavy hair. Around the circle it said, Starbucks.

"What is this?" I asked.

"Carmel Macchiato," he said as he sat down. "I wasn't sure you were a coffee drinker and that's more like candy than coffee." He smiled. "Careful, it has whipped cream."

Did he know about me and whipped cream? I looked up at him, but he was staring at the wall above my head. When I turned, I saw a green and blue painting of a lake with white mist rising off the water.

I blurted out, "Merriman is a character in a book."

He looked at me with an odd expression and then grinned. "Yeah, I've read them. Only I don't have the magic that Merriman does."

"Doing magic could be cool," I said thinking of Harry Potter and how he could wear his father's invisibility cloak and get anywhere he wanted.

Merriman got a gleam in his eye and he said, "But I can fly."

"Huh?" I said still holding my untried drink. I had attempted a couple of times, but was afraid of burning my mouth.

"Yeah, see?" He put his cup down on the wooden table. He pulled his wallet out of his back pocket and took out a picture. He handed it over to me. The photo was of Merriman, in midair with only sky behind him. He had on mirrored sunglasses, black gloves and jeans. His blond hair was peaking out behind a black fleece hat. He was on a snowboard and one of his black gloved hands was giving the thumbs up.

"Whoa," I said. "That's really cool."

"Too bad the guy who took it was lying on the snow under me, huh?" He chuckled. "Almost landed on him." He put the picture back in his wallet and his wallet back in his pocket.

In my dreams I could fly. Not just falling. Flying. I could soar around like Superman, only my arms were out to the side instead of straight up by my ears. It was more like I was on a cross. I hovered about three or four feet above the earth and could feel the wind soar through my hair and my body was filled with some unknown power. Then some idiot teacher, or dumb friend always tried to teach me how to fly. They said, "Well, you start like this, and leap like this and you're off." And then, I couldn't do it anymore. I crashed to the earth, scraping my chin, leaving blood everywhere. I awoke bitter and disappointed, not because I once flew, but because someone who thought they were really helping me ruined my ability. I didn't tell Merriman any of this.

"How did you know I was asking about you?" I said moving the conversation forward.

He took a sip of his coffee. And then another. "What do you want to know?"

I decided to be brutal. "Are you good enough for my sister?"

"Is your sister good enough for me?" he asked.

I almost lynched him, but he continued, "Or, am I really no good and not worth the coffee I'm drinking."

"Exactly." I braved a sip of the cup I was holding. It was sweet and creamy.

"Why would I bring you out here?" Merriman asked.

You're a freak? "I have no idea." I replied.

"No, I'm not worth your sister in some ways. Nor is she worth me in others."

"Why did you bring me out here?" I asked.

"Told you already. I think it's good for you to be around normal guys, not that freak brother of yours."

"Suppose you're the freak," I said before I could stop

myself.

"Maybe I am the freak. Maybe I am the one who's all messed up. But you are the one who agreed to come here and you seem to really like the coffee."

"Right."

"So, who's the freak?" he asked.

"Me," I said. "I am definitely a freak."

He laughed outright. That made me crack up. I grinned like a lunatic for a while afterwards and we finished our coffee.

***

Zeke was in the kitchen when Merriman dropped me off. "Poppy will make you sleep," Zeke said.

I grunted at him and bit my tongue. I could feel my body coursing with caffeine and I knew enough to shut my mouth and try to squeak past him to my room.

"She called," he teased. "Said she needed tonight's math homework. I think she wanted more."

"Whatever," I said.

"Where were you, if you weren't with her?"

"Up your butt, Zeke, and you're constipated."

He slammed me into the wall but I bounced to freedom, and laughed my way up the stairs.

***

The following Tuesday afternoon I was sitting at the scary white kitchen table at the Rabbi's house. "So did you practice?" Mrs. Cohn, the rabbi's wife asked.

I could have lied; I could have been honest and said no. Instead I said nothing and held out the slip of paper that proved I had been to Friday night services, a requirement to continue being tutored and tutoring was a requirement for my Bar Mitzvah. Really, the system was so connected the only way I could get out of *any* of it was to not have the Bar Mitzvah at all, but that would bring shame upon my whole family. If I could just bring shame to Zeke, that would be one thing. But to tell the truth, if I didn't have the Bar Mitzvah, Grey, Mom and Dad would feel the shame. Zeke wouldn't care. So the one I would want to hurt the most would be hurt the least and the ones I would want to hurt the least would hurt the most. I was having a Bar Mitzvah, I admit, for the money and for my family. Not for God. Not for my faith, which I was dead sure didn't exist.

***

Grey's lost it. Really. She's gone. I heard her on the phone last night. I was outside her bedroom door, sitting against the white wood on the blue carpet; periwinkle, Mom calls it. I pictured Grey lounging in her black butterfly chair, leaning back like a model, dancing her brown wavy hair over the edge to be licked by the air. She was on the phone with Merriman, I knew because she only giggles like that when she's on the phone with a guy she really likes.

I heard her say, "But how did Jesus become a man, if he's God?"

Another pause, this one longer.

"...I still don't get it.... No, it makes sense, sort of, but...."

A long pause.

"Uh-huh - I know, but this is bizarre stuff you're talking about."

I wanted to yell through the door, "Grey! We're Jewish!" But I bit my tongue and pushed my ear harder to the door until it began to throb, which drowned out any words she might be saying.

***

Maybe I was the one who'd lost it because I brought it up at my Rabbi's kitchen table. You know, the one where the Rabbi comes to eat in his blue striped pajamas and where he reads the newspaper every morning. It still smelled like Jewish chicken noodle soup, a matzo ball or two and perhaps a hint of latkahs, or as most people know them, potato pancakes.

I looked at Mrs. Cohn, my heart racing, my fingers making the papers in front of me damp as I fiddled with the corners and kept folding them on their creases weakening the paper each time. I opened my snake-dry lips and said it. "Who was Jesus Christ?"

She stared at me. What Paddington would call, "a hard stare." I thought she wanted to catapult me out of my chair, out the front windows in her living room. Her steel-plated stare made me feel like I was one of those nasty silverfish with billions of legs that they lose when, by a tissue, the life gets squished out of them.

She looked down at the paper I was fiddling with. It was my Torah portion, now yellowed and dirty from all of the use I'd been giving it. In reality, I just touched it a lot and once I intentionally touched it right after being out in the woods with Poppy and Matters to make it look good and worn.

"Jesus was a prophet. Did you study?"

"Yes," I said. *Once.*

"Good. So read your portion all the way through."

I started to struggle through the back of the throat garglings of Hebrew when Mrs. Cohn stopped me.

"You didn't really practice, did you?"

"Once," I replied, knowing how lame it sounded.

She sighed and her eyebrows crinkled together as she looked at me. "This needs to come from you," she said. "I can't force you to do this. You need to care about it on your own."

"Was Jesus God?" I asked again, almost cutting her off.

"No," she said.

"Then what was he?"

"Just really smart. Now, have you started the essay?" Her mouth was pinched in a way I had never seen.

"No."

"I would like you to have the rough draft next week." She handed me a piece of paper with a bunch of bulleted statements. "These are the requirements."

I couldn't give it up. I didn't care how mad she got.

"Why don't we believe in him? He was Jewish, wasn't he?"

"Yes, but he wasn't God."

"How do people know he isn't?"

"How do people know he is?" she said, even more stern—like it was a warning not to ask any more. The next time I tried to walk into her house, she might slam the door shut in my face. She might tell me I'm no longer Jewish. Or that I'm a disgrace to Judaism, and I should be sent out of camp with only spitting camels for companions as I wander aimless like the Israelites before they got into the Promised Land. I took the essay requirements and made up my mind to ask Merriman.

I left the table weak-kneed about ten minutes later, when my mom arrived to pick me up. She rang the doorbell and Mrs. Cohn, who hadn't stopped boring her eyes into me said, "Go. Go home. Study and I want a much better session next week. I don't appreciate having my time wasted."

I was a really bad Jew.

***

Matters and I were walking down the hall in school toward the front doors and freedom, when Merriman caught up with us. "Wondering if you want coffee," he said.

"I would like that. I've been thinking about that Macchiato stuff way too much."

"You can come along," he said to Matters.

I tried to say that Matters had too much homework and all, with his fencing lessons, but it didn't work.

"I have no idea what you're talking about," Matters said following us to the parking lot.

Once in Merriman's Jeep, Matters started to make fun of Merriman's music. It was a little different from the rocking stuff he had played before, this had stringed instruments and lots of bass. "Rain, Rain on my face," were only a few of the lines I caught before Merriman turned it off to humor Matters. I could have punched Matters, but decided to ignore him, instead.

"Dude, you and your sister have got some serious stuff to work out," Merriman said after I told him about the scene I had made in the Rabbi's house the day before.

I grunted.

We sat down at a long wooden table toward the front of the shop.

One sip from the paper cup with the plastic lid; it was better than I remembered, all smooth and sweet, only I wanted some so fast, and with all the whipped cream, I forgot about how hot it could be. My mouth was on fire and my tongue became numb.

Matters and Merriman had started an argument about God in the car. I had tried to follow it, but I got lost in the "original sin" part. Once we were seated, Matters picked it up where they left off.

"God doesn't work that way," Matters said.

"What way?" Merriman sounded serious and sincere in his interest.

Matters was getting serious, too. "Like, involvement in your life. He's just there. You know, judging."

"How's snowboarding?" I asked trying to change the subject.

Merriman ignored my question. "I don't think He's judging."

I looked down into the tiny hole in the white lid to the frothiness below.

Merriman waited. Matters stared at him in disbelief. I could feel his back getting up. Believe me, I've known the kid forever. When he gets going, he radiates tension like the space heater in Dad's study lets off swarming hotness.

The coffee shop smelled of rich grounds. Ella Fitzgerald's "Mack the Knife," pumped down at us. The whooshing of the espresso maker foaming milk for cappuccino was in the background and the sunlight overwhelmed the glow the lamps tried to shine down from above.

I cut Matters off. "Look. God is untouchable. I don't even know why we are talking about Him. I mean, like He even exists."

Merriman sipped his coffee. Matters looked shocked.

"And," I said, "I'm not supposed to be saying this. I'm just supposed to follow along and do what a good Bar Mitzvah is supposed to do. Don't complain. Jump through this hoop. Now jump higher. Good dog, have a thousand dollars."

"Have you told anyone about your feelings?" Merriman asked.

I shook my head. "Maybe. But when I ask, I feel like, well, they are all too busy. They don't have time for my thoughts. I wanted to learn Hebrew, so that I really knew it. I didn't just want to pronounce the prayers, but I wanted to understand what I was saying. I was told they didn't have time to teach me. So, now, I don't let them know what I'm thinking; I just do what I'm told."

Merriman was quiet for a long time and then said, "Where does Grey fit in?"

"She's asking what I've been thinking."

"Like what?" he asked.

"Why would God love me," I replied watching a couple in matching tan London Fog raincoats walk in. It was sunny out....

"Is God's love any harder to understand as a Jew than it would be for a Christian?" he asked.

"I wouldn't know. I'm not a Christian."

"God doesn't love us; He judges us," Matters said.

Merriman leaned forward toward Matters, who was all scrawny and slouched down in his chair. "That's not how I see it," said Merriman.

"How's it for you?" Matters said with a sharp knife flashing in his voice.

"Love. He takes me how I am and brings me to where He wants me to be. No judgment, just love."

"Then you and I know two different Jesuses," Matters said.

"No." Merriman said, his blond snowboarding hair falling into his eyes. "You and I have two different religions."

"Can God love me?" I said feeling way confused.

"Not as a Jew," Matters said.

I sipped my drink and didn't even notice the deep sweetness.

Merriman fixed Matters with a deep penetrating glare, like the Rabbi's wife gave to me. Then Merriman turned to me and said, "With Jesus you don't have to *do* anything. He looks at your heart and that is enough."

Matters snorted into his coffee. I let what Merriman said seep in. When I looked at him, he was staring at me. Not in the catapult way the Rabbi's wife had, but in a concerned kind of way. "Thank you," I whispered and Merriman raised his coffee cup to me and finished his last swallow.

Matters was pouting, slunked down even further in his chair. He had turned and was staring at the cars turning into the parking lot. When Merriman started to stand up, Matters didn't look at either of us. He threw his white cup out like the rest of us and trailed us to the car.

I sat shotgun on the way home and turned up the volume so much the speakers pounded out Jars of Clay.

***

When I walked into the family room at the end of the day, and plunked down my bookbag, Zeke didn't even look up from the glowing TV. He grunted around the house, sulked in chairs, didn't fight for the remote, and ignored me when I came near him. I hadn't seen a hamster, a rodent or a jellybean in weeks and this ignoring me was making me kind of edgy. Like, maybe he had this big secret attack planned. What if he took a can of Reddi-Whip, grabbed me from behind in the blue and white checkered floored hallway? What if he shoved it in the top of my pants and sprayed all that gooey smoothness? Where could I hide? What if Michelle saw? Or worse, what if Poppy noticed how it affected me?

When I approached Grey about my fears she said that Zeke was scared because he had no future.

"Why not?" I asked.

"He's stupid?" she said, flopping into Mom's chair. Then she said, "As a junior, I already have a list of colleges, and visits lined up. I'm planning ahead. Finding out what I need to get on my S.A.T.'s and I'm in the process of convincing Mom and Dad to sign me up now for a course on how to take them. Zeke did okay on his, but not well enough to get into the good schools."

"Oh," I said turning away from the glowing computer screen to her. The blue glow made her face like what you imagine a ghost would look like.

"He came into my room the other day with the mail. He had this stupid look. 'Bard,' he said. 'What's Bard?' I almost laughed in his face."

Even I knew Grey had been considering Bard and had recently declared at dinner that it was her first choice school. Zeke was at the table and he didn't even hear the whole discussion of why.

"Maybe he didn't care until now." I swiveled in the navy blue office chair I was sitting in.

"Seems like that talk with Dad really did something to him," Grey said. "He hasn't insulted me in days, hasn't picked on you, nor has he tried to ask Michelle out again."

"Huh?" I said. "I didn't know Zeke was still interested in her."

"He *hates* when she stops to talk to you." Grey laughed out loud and it rang around the room.

"See, normal Zeke would have let me know in no uncertain terms how he felt."

Grey became serious again, "Agreed."

"What's he going to do?"

"I don't know, but if I were you," Grey said, "I would avoid him when he changes from being depressed to being angry. Zeke angry isn't a pretty sight."

"I don't look forward to it."

Grey and I sat in silence for a few moments. The windows were dark black but for the white spot of a full moon.

"How are you doing?" I asked.

"Lots on my mind."

"Agreed."

"How's the Bar Mitzvah stuff?" she asked.

"I'm supposed to write this essay, but I haven't a clue what to write."

"What's your portion on?" She dug her long bare toes into the plush beige carpet. The section of Torah you have to read at your Bar Mitzvah is called your Torah portion or just portion.

Before I could answer, she said, "I had a whole bunch of laws, like don't have idols above God. In that list was one about keeping the Sabbath holy. I talked about the Sabbath and how we, as Reform Jews, see the Sabbath and what a day set apart for God should look like."

She stopped talking and looked at me. "And what did you wind up with?"

"Kosher laws - you know - clean and unclean animals." I turned sideways back and forth, back and forth, back and forth in the chair.

"You love to eat, that could be a fun angle," Grey

suggested.

"Crustaceans aren't clean. That means we can't eat shrimp or lobster."

"Speak for yourself, Buster," Grey frowned. "I'll eat all the clams I want."

"But if they're not clean, then you're not clean and you have to make sacrifices to God to get clean again. *Or* we have to send you out of camp." I pictured her stranded, alone in the desert with no one to talk to, except her spitting camel. Miles and miles of yellow sand and she would be reclining on an oriental carpet.

Grey laughed. "Send Zeke out of camp."

I liked the suggestion. He was unclean.

* * *

Poppy stopped me at my locker. She was playing with her hair, one dark thick braid, twirling it around her finger. The bubble of the gum she was chewing made her breath smell like a candy cane. She had on a short tight green skirt, gray and white argyle tights and little black shoes.

"S'up?" I said, trying to sound normal.

"I should ask you that."

"So, you still mad?" I said. She popped the bubble she was blowing, and then leaned against the locker next to mine and dropped her bookbag at her feet.

"I'm sorry if I said something to offend you." I shoved my English textbook in my bag and slung it over my shoulder. I couldn't look at her, just her legs and shoes.

"It cracks me up you still don't get it." Poppy shook her head; she looked at me like I was nuts: her forehead crinkled, a half grin pulling at one side of her face and giving a hint of her dimples.

"I've missed you," I said.

"I thought you were having too much fun going to coffee with Merriman."

"Yeah, but it's not the same." How could I tell Poppy that I missed the way I felt when she was next to me? I missed the way she made me smile, even if I was mad at her. I loved the way she smelled when she wasn't wearing perfume, and when she was, I loved the way she made my knees wobble as I secretly took deep whiffs hoping my shirt would smell like her at the end of the day. I loved how depressed I was when I got home, took off my shirt, inhaled, and only smelled my own sweat.

We were walking down the stuffy white and blue linoleum floor toward the open doorway of homeroom 124B.

"Merriman has the info on stuff like God," I said, "and religions no Jew should be asking about."

"You could ask me," Poppy said as she dodged a boy in a white T-shirt that he wore tucked into massive orange jeans held up by a belt. He was running so fast his blue and white flannel was flapping. After he passed, the smell of cologne lingered.

"I know," I said.

But the thought of talking to Poppy about God was like going to the dentist for drilling. It gave me the chills. My mouth filled up with saliva faster than the sucker could inhale all the spit. Besides, Poppy often agreed with Matters when they talked about religion. For some reason I couldn't figure out, Merriman was different.

***

That afternoon, I walked into the family room to pick up a copy of *Newsweek* that was sitting next to the sofa. My social studies teacher wanted us to find an article about the modern day Middle East since we were just about to leave the ancient times in that area and he wanted to talk about what was going on there today.

I had to cross in front of Zeke to get it and when I did he said, "You know, you wouldn't be so bad looking if you cut your hair a little shorter."

My hair was getting long I will admit that. And when it gets a little long, it starts to curl around my face and into my eyes.

"Listen Zeke, you wouldn't be so bad looking if you lost a little weight."

I got the mountain to move. The boy who had been sulking, slumping in sofas and grunting out orders, looked up. He moved in a solid swift motion upwards, leaned in toward me and fell on top of me. I didn't even see him sway. He just reached out, grabbed my arm and smeared me into the carpet. I couldn't breathe.

Then, when I could breathe again, I looked up, and started to check each limb to see if it worked properly without too much pain. I glanced up at the couch. Zeke, in his athletic pants and oversized sweatshirt, was sunk in the sofa, with his back sloped against the seat; the remote was in his hand and he flicked through channels.

***

I was sitting at the breakfast bar in the kitchen when Grey walked through to the laundry room to get a bottle of water. That's where Mom stores the vast quantities of stuff she buys at Costco. She came back into the kitchen, snapped off the protective clear cap, pulled up on the drinking spout and swooshed a bit into her mouth.

"Why do you let him do it?" she asked as I held a bag of frozen corn to my chin in the hope of not getting a black and blue mark.

"I don't ask for it. I just don't back down."

"Maybe you should," Grey said pulling the white bag of corn away from my face to survey the damage.

"If I give in a little, he'll never back down." I pulled my chin away and grabbed the bag from her hand and shoved it back on my face, wincing a little as the cold spread. "Why doesn't he ever pick on you?"

"Doesn't need to. I don't compete with him." She leaned forward and placed her elbows on the white counter. She placed her head in her hands and cupped her face in her fingers, her bum up in the air.

"He's a senior. I'm in the seventh grade, not even close to being a freshman," I said.

"No, at many things you're above him. Don't you think *he* notices that?"

I couldn't look her in those deep green eyes, instead I started to smush the one or two sesame seeds left from someone's bagel that morning.

"He could leave me alone; I'm family - his little brother. Isn't he supposed to protect me or something?"

"Oh," Grey said, "from an outsider he would protect you, but here, inside the house, you're the hunted."

"Couldn't you pull rank and help me out?"

Grey thought a moment, tugged the parts of her long hair that curled into her eyes and put them behind her ears, not taking her elbows off the counter. "Why take sides? Be like Switzerland, you know? Neutral."

"So you are choosing to be neutral in the middle of a European war zone. Some people could call that noble and courageous; I call that cowardly and pathetic."

Her eyebrows came together and she frowned at me. She gets that look when animals are hurt on TV or when she doesn't get to have olives on her Friday night pizza. I ignored her expression and continued. "If you don't stand up against what is wrong, you become a part of the problem. By allowing it to occur -- you are saying it's okay."

Grey shook her head. "That's not true."

"Look at the Jews in Germany," I said. "If you didn't stand against the Nazis, you were for the Nazis."

"I think you're blowing this a little out of proportion," Grey said. "This is Zeke. Your brother. He's not a Nazi."

"No? Think about it, Grey. If you're Switzerland, what does that make him?"

Her eyebrows came together even more and she lifted her head out of her hands, raised herself up and turned away from me to the refrigerator. With the door open, she said, "Don't let Mom and Dad hear you talking this way."

I had learned about the silence when we went to a holocaust memorial in Miami, Florida. We went to the memorials, got really close to the green metal statues of little people of bone people, and wept in their faces. We wept for those who no longer are able to weep and then we left. The sun was still shining. The heat was still oppressive. My throat was tight and my eyes burned because I would not allow myself to weep. I forced myself to be like those silenced. We went to the memorial and when we got out, we went immediately looking for lunch, a good kanish, bagels and lox. Anything that showed our Judaism, but we only whispered nondescriptive words like, "That was hard," or "That was beautiful," because anything louder or more meaningful cut raw flesh, bone and sinew.

Grey glared at me. "That's wrong," she snapped and slammed the refrigerator behind her.

"What?" I asked taking the corn down from my chin.

"To call your brother a Nazi. That's so harsh and.... I don't even have words for it," she snapped, and then grabbed her water bottle off the counter. She ran out of the kitchen with her brown hair bouncing on her gray sweater as she fled.

***

We were in math and Poppy's head was bent over Algebra. She was chewing on the side of her cheek and her forehead was crinkled in concentration. Her hair was all up in a braided bun, thick and bulging, and she was gripping her pencil so hard her knuckles were white.

"Poppy?"

"Hmm?" she asked.

"What do I do?"

"Stop talking," Mrs. Alberta ordered.

I frowned up at the old bat with her wrinkled leather face and squinty-eyed bat scowl. She was sitting behind her little round table at the front of the room grading papers. When Mrs. Alberta was distracted by the papers in front of her again, I whispered to Poppy, "Well?"

She ignored me, her head hunched over her own paper.

"Just answer," I said.

"Stop!" Mrs. Alberta yelled. "I'll take your papers and give you zeros."

"Poppy?"

"Will you shush?" she whispered back. "Ask me later."

I reigned my racing mind back in and put my head over my math paper.

$2x + 3y = 30y - 12x$ Solve for x if $y = 1$

This was not going to be easy.

***

Merriman had met up with me at my locker during the break after lunch. "You up for the ride of your life?"

"Does this involve snow?" I asked a little nervous.

He thought for a moment. "No, but it could. Except, there isn't any snow yet."

"Good point," I said. "I don't have the clothes for it."

"One day perhaps," he said. "It could be way fun."

So, at his Jeep, after I had hopped in and he put on Switchfoot, he said, "Anything on your mind?"

"How did you know?" I asked.

"Just a suspicion," he replied as he turned out of the student parking lot, the opposite way most people go.

"Where we going?" I asked.

"You'll see," he said and glanced over at me. Then he laughed and said, "Relax. What's your question?"

"Does...or I should say, did. Did Jesus love the Nazis?" I asked it in such a low voice that I barely heard myself over the pumping bass.

Merriman had heard me, though. He looked up from the road and glanced at me again and then looked back, letting the question sink in. He exhaled hard; his shoulders dropped. "Alex, this is a hard one."

"I know."

My head was beginning to ring. I felt like I did when I had a shot of penicillin for pneumonia in the fifth grade when I couldn't swallow the pills anymore because they made my stomach so upset I had stopped eating. We were passing the woods with its browns and greens deepened by the morning rain and fog; the trees weren't as intriguing as the constantness of the double yellow line. Could God love such hateful people?

"Yes," Merriman replied at last. "God loves the Nazis, just not what they did."

If God could love a Nazi, then I wouldn't be as hard to love. But it hurt to think that a Nazi could be in heaven. How could God allow a Nazi in? We are His Chosen People. You don't just let someone into heaven who goes after God's Chosen Ones. That just doesn't make sense. Think of heaven, all bright white, silky and glowing golden and add an olive green Gestapo uniform. It doesn't fit; they don't belong.

I told Merriman so and he said, "God sees into the hearts of men. He's the one who judges us. What He decides may or may not make sense to us. We need to trust that He knows what He's doing. My gut says there's no way Hitler's heart could have been right with God. But some of his men may have really repented and turned their lives over to Christ. Of course, they would still have to suffer the consequences of their wrong actions in this world, but they could make it into heaven."

The double yellow line continued past; we headed deeper into the woods.

***

You can't take Michelle or Poppy out of a dream. They're in there and you can't really touch them, you just have to pray that your dream is enough to make it feel like you're touching them. In my sleep, Poppy allows me to hold her hand, kiss her mouth, her neck, her collar bone. Her stomach shivers under my touch and her ribs inch my hands upward.

Of course, in the morning I wake up to a mess and I blush when I see her, but in my dream, she was real, alive and she wanted me. There were no blushes, no moments of embarrassment when I felt her legs and found out how strong her arms were in my dream. But in the hallway, surrounded by classmates and middle schoolers, and screaming teachers who really don't want you to have a life, I blushed and asked her, "How was your night?"

"Boring," she said with an odd look toward the boy who had his pants down so far, they were below his butt, his flannel plaid boxers were exposed and the belt holding it all up was slipping. "And your night?" she asked, prying her eyes away.

"Don't ask." How was possible that she didn't dream what I did? It was so real. How could she *not* have had the dream too?

"Well, did you finish the math homework?" she asked.

I hit myself on the forehead and trundled off to homeroom to save myself from one of Mrs. Alberta's dreaded zeros.

***

I wanted to read that weird language, Hebrew, and know all of its parts - like an algebra problem. I asked. I asked my Hebrew school teacher in the fifth grade if the Hebrew we were reading was translated in the italicized English below it, and she said, "No." I already suspected that. The Hebrew word for "Israel" would be in the Hebrew passage, but the word, "Israel," wouldn't be in any of the English anywhere below that Hebrew.

"Can you teach me to read this?" I asked pointing to the Hebrew passage.

"No," she said looking from my prayer book to me.

"What?" I asked, a little frustrated.

"We don't have time."

I just looked at her as she started to fill her bag.

"We don't have enough classtime to teach you actual Hebrew. We only have time to teach you to read the prayers."

"Can anyone teach me this?" I asked and pointed again to the Hebrew on the page.

She shook her head. "We are all busy. Most of us have full-time jobs. We don't have the time."

No one has time for you.

I hate having to go into the Rabbi's office to talk to him about my Bar Mitzvah. He has a whole synagogue to worry about, and I'm just an almost 13-year old boy. He has more important things to be attending to, like meetings, marriages, and the other things. Not chatting to some zit-covered, whiny twelve year old who isn't certain he's a Jew.

And sitting at the Rabbi's kitchen table every week makes me shake. My knees bounce up and down so I swear they'll hit the bottom of the table. My palms sweat and my tongue swells so that even when I *have* practiced, the Hebrew won't come out right. What right do I have to be in the Rabbi's house, at his table, spending time with his wife? Doesn't she have more important things to be doing?

Does that make God too busy?

***

Merriman met up with Matters and me as we pushed our

way to our lockers after last block's study hall.

"Okay," Merriman said. "God loves everyone, tall, short, happy, sad, awkward and zit-covered. He loves everyone."

"I get it; He loves Nazis. Everybody gets into heaven." I said it in the harshest tone I could; the idea of *them*, all olive green, contaminating heaven made my skin shake like a cobra trying to molt.

"Yes, but they won't be in heaven if they don't love Him back."

"What?" I said. "Merriman, this doesn't make sense."

"Nazi's should burn in hell," Matters said as he slumped down the hall with us.

"Maybe you should too," Merriman said with anger in his voice. I could tell he said it without thinking. Merriman turned red and closed his mouth.

"Why?" Matters was offended. "I go to church, I know the sacraments, I take communion. I go to confession and I'm going to heaven."

"Suppose a Nazi did the *exact* same thing?" Merriman asked. "Would they go to heaven?"

Matters was quiet.

"What makes you different?" I needed to understand this. "I mean, I know you're not Nazi, but why do you think you're different from Matters?"

Merriman had gotten back to his cool, calm self. "Matters has all these rituals that a bunch of men say will get him closer to God. I just go directly to God—it's like going right up to the person you have a crush on, instead of going to her best-friend's good friend and hope that she gets the message and will like you back."

Matters pouted. "That's not how I see it."

"I can accept that."

"Does God even know me?" I asked.

"Of course," Merriman replied.

"How do you know that?" I asked.

"What has Hebrew school taught you?" He was looking at me while relying on his peripheral vision to dodge other kids trying to get down the hallway in the opposite direction.

"I've been taugh that, um, that we're the Chosen Ones and

that the Torah, the first five books, Genesis, Exodus, Leviticus, Numbers and Deuteronomy, aren't *really* the words of God. Just smart men wrote down wise words and we get to decide what we're going to follow."

"So there isn't anything you really believe as a Jew?" Merriman stopped midstream in the hallway causing a log-jam behind us. People jostled past him muttering and pushing his shoulders. He just stood there and let himself be plowed.

"Yes," I said feeling uncomfortable and stepping forward in the hopes to get Merriman walking again. "We believe we're the Chosen Ones of the only living God."

"The Chosen Ones who missed it," Matters said.

"Ugh! Matters, you are so insensitive!" Merriman snapped.

"They did," he said.

"You don't get it either, but you don't hear me telling you you're wrong."

"You just did," I pointed out.

"I was provoked," Merriman said, his face red in frustration.

Matters frowned. "Merriman, why don't you respect my opinion?"

"Because you don't respect Alex's questioning," he replied. "And because you teach a bad version of God."

"You're such a bastard," Matters said.

Merriman looked right in Matters' eyes as he walked, but didn't say anything. Matters was walking in the middle and I was on the other side. The look even knocked the wind out of me. It wasn't harsh or cruel. It was open and hurt. It was almost like he was inviting another insult.

"What about God knowing me?" I asked.

"Alex," he said, directing his words past Matters and still walking forward. People moved to get out of his way, not everybody succeeded. "God knows *everything* about you and everything that's important to you. He knows all that stuff you don't want to reveal to *anyone* and, this is important," he said, "He loves you despite that stuff."

"That doesn't make sense." But inside I felt my stomach jump. He knew all of the stuff I never shared with anyone. He knew about my dreams, whipped cream and about how I really thought about Poppy?

"He's God. He doesn't have to make sense."

This was insane. I was worried about what God knew about me, and I was not even certain God existed. We continued down the hallway to our lockers in silence. I started to work the combination on my black and white numbered lock, Merriman stopped with me. Matters was far down at his locker, but still Merriman whispered, "You up for coffee?"

"Absolutely."

***

Mrs. Cohn started the next tutoring session by saying, "Now, let me see that essay."

I produced a white sheet of paper that had typed marks running in lines across it. The marks were letters forming words forming sentences forming ideas.

It was not an essay about clean and unclean animals. It was an essay about God, His love and His desire to be with His people, so He made kosher laws to keep His people close to Him.

Mrs. Cohn read it, her dark eyebrows pulled together forming a crease between them on her forehead. She made a couple of notes and looked up, with a smile.

I grinned back, but it was only my face that smiled. My stomach, like when Merriman said that God could see my thoughts, was rolling and foaming because every word I wrote in that essay was a lie.

***

I had just sat down at the computer to check my e-mail—mostly junk and a few blathering lines from Matters about the science project that wasn't due for a month and a half—when Grey came into the study and shut the door. She sat down in Mom's swallowing floral chair and sighed. I had not bothered to turn on any lights when I came in, and so we were sitting in the blue glow of the computer monitor.

I was in the navy blue office chair and stayed focused on the computer screen. I glanced at her once, but didn't know what to do with the strained look on her face that the computer made more wrinkled.

"You talk to Merriman recently?"

"Yeah," I said as I read about some new deal at Barnes and Noble to get 10% off every purchase. Why do I get this stuff? *Blah, blah, blah.* I punched good old "control D"—and it was gone.

"Why?" I asked as I read a couple of lines from Poppy about plans for the weekend.

She was silent.

"What's up?" I asked not really wanting to but forcing myself to swivel and really look at her for the first time. She stared at the floor and I watched, shocked, as two tears dropped down her cheeks.

My jaw opened a little, my mind raced for what to say. Nothing useful. So I sat in silence watching the glittering blue crystals fall from her eyes, slip down her cheeks, gather near her chin and drop with small splotches onto her jeans.

Her hair was pulled back in a messy bun. Some strands had become loose in front with many wisps around her eyes, which she often tucked behind her ears.

I grabbed a tissue and shoved it at her. My tongue was still slammed, unusable, in the car door of my teeth.

"I'm sorry," she muttered. "I'm so lost and I thought you would understand."

"Maybe," my throat said surprising my brain.

"I'm really struggling with this God thing." She looked up from the floor for the first time. There were light blue flecks from the monitor reflected in her eyes. I could feel the pain and confusion coming off of her, toppling me off my chair. As my stomach lurched for what seemed the fourth time that day, I thought that maybe I should ask Mom to make a doctor's appointment for me.

"What has Mrs. Cohn told you?" she asked.

"Nothing satisfying."

"What do you mean?"

I remembered Mrs. Cohn's harsh tone telling me Jesus wasn't God. "She just said he was really smart. A prophet," I said and swiveled my seat. Left, right, left, right. Slow. Not knowing how to help her.

Grey's tears still fell. "Jews are looking for a political king, change. Peace in Israel."

"Not going to happen," I said with a shake of my head, trying to sound comforting.

"Not with the Mosque," Grey added as a few more tears slipped out. She wiped the crystals away with the back of her hand.

In Jerusalem, the chosen city, where the Jews believe the temple used to be, is a large blue building with a gold dome that reflects light everywhere. Inside is a Muslim sanctuary, a Muslim place of worship. Not, as it once was, a place for God to dwell. At least, that's what Mrs. Cohn said about a year ago to our Hebrew school class.

"You know, I learned in Hebrew school that they think the Holy of Holies is under that Mosque," I said.

I had been taught that the Holy of Holies was where the priest went to offer sacrifices to God. He only went in one day a year, and if he wasn't clean, then God would strike him dead upon entering. They said that he had a rope tied around his waist and put many bells on his robe so that if the bells stopped ringing, they would know he died before God. Using the rope, they would drag his sorry butt out. I would hate to have that job. Talk about high risk.

Grey shook her head. "It's not possible that the Mosque is over the Holy of Holies. They would be killed."

"Unless they were found pleasing before the Lord."

"Like anyone building the Mosque would be pleasing to God."

"Maybe if they were doing what God wanted," I said, thinking aloud. "Or if the ark wasn't there, would they still be struck down?"

"Who could walk in and pick up the ark without being struck down?" she asked. "You've seen *Raiders of the Lost Ark*, you know what God does to those who don't do as He wants."

"I think...," I said and then, after actually stopping to think said, "I don't know."

"Me neither," she looked at me, blue and glowing in the computer's light. "Was Jesus God?"

"Not according to Mrs. Cohn."

"Yeah, but she's *Jewish*. Like married-to-the-Rabbi, Jewish," she said.

"What would Mom and Dad say if they could hear us?"

"This isn't about them. This is about truth."

***

Poppy's head was bent over an Algebra problem as we sat in her bedroom and she went over how do the latest assignment with me. She had on a black scooped neck T-shirt with a pale pink button-down sweater over top. She was exposing that muscle, you know? The one that forms a triangle in the front at the neck's base? The one that made me want to lean forward and touch her....

"It's not that big a deal," Poppy said. "You take what's on one side and do the opposite to the other."

"So, I don't get it," my mouth said to drive my mind away from what she would taste like.

"Were you paying attention?" she asked, irritated.

I could feel the heat rise to my face, but I said, "Yeah, but I'm thick. Can you do it again?" I ignored her sigh of frustration and allowed my head to almost touch hers as we leaned over the same notebook.

***

Hours later, I was making a sandwich, ham and cheese with lettuce and hot mustard, in the kitchen.

"Speak to me in Hebrew," Zeke said as he stuck his head in the kitchen doorway from the family room.

"What?" I said looking at his fat face.

"Give me what I want," he purred as he reached a meaty hand toward me. His eyes were wide and his face was in a toothy grin like they have hanging up in dentist's offices. He was in his flopping jeans and a cotton sweater that had a hole in the sleeve. Mom hated that sweater, and tried to get rid of it at least twice a year. Zeke claimed it was his favorite and so he wore it all the time. I think he just did it to see Mom turn red and sputter.

"Get out of here, Fat Ass," I muttered as I turned back to the counter and put the two pieces of whole wheat bread together.

"What did you call me?"

"Fat Ass, Chipmunk Brains, Jockstrap Nose, Snot Fingers...," I said.

He stormed the room. I could hear his boots hitting the floor hard and my back became straight as I prepared for his impact. I don't know why I thought the deer in the headlights technique, stand still and stare, was going to help. Always at the last second, I change my mind and try to take off--*fast*

I tried to run, but he grabbed my pants in the back. My sandwich clutched in my hands. Zeke held on, not to my jeans, but to my freaking flannel boxers.

I twisted, spun so fast in mad circles until he had to loosen his grip. I was free, off and dizzy, slipping and spinning over the white linoleum floor into the white counters.

I slammed to a stop by the cabinets. Zeke grabbed my sandwich and ate the whole thing in one bite. "Thanks," he said trying to chew, bread sticking out the sides and front of his mouth.

I watched his saggy pants leave and grabbed the loaf of wheat bread that I left out on the counter.

"Get a life," I muttered as I started to smear hot mustard on the wheat bread.

***

Dad and I were on our Saturday night drive for pizzas: pepperoni, meatball and garlic. Yum. Good thing we didn't keep kosher where no meat and dairy can touch each other.

As Dad drove 80 mph, each white dot zoomed behind us like they had someplace important to go. His hands were resting on the black thick steering wheel. One thumb tapped out the beat the classical station was pumping out.

"Dad?"

"Hmmm?" He did not look over at me. "What's on your mind?"

"Nothing really." A lie. A big fat LIE, spoken with liar breath and a lying lizard tongue.

Dad glanced at me. His eyes flickered across my face which I worked really hard to remain blank. Show nothing, reveal *nothing*.

"How are you, Alex?"

"How are you?" I countered.

"Well," he said through a sigh, "work is challenging. My boss has told me I'm up for another promotion. Thing is, I like what I do and a promotion would mean I'll have to do stuff I don't really like. But more money would be good with all you guys thinking about college."

"I'm not thinking about college," I said staring out the window into the night that was almost dark. The sky was a deep mystical blue, the way Grey's favorite artist, Maxfield Parish, paints his skies.

"You're not thinking about college yet," he said, laughing. "But soon, you will be."

"Not soon enough," I said.

"You won't believe how fast the time goes by. For me, your birth was like four days ago. Just boom. Before I knew it, you were in middle school, fighting with your brother and looking out for Grey."

I looked over at his Jewish nose and wondered if my nose would look like his one day with that little bump on the bridge. They say that noses never stop growing, which would explain why my grandfather's is so huge.

"I'm glad you turned out so thoughtful and caring," he continued still keeping his eyes on the road, his left arm leaning on the car door, against the window. His right hand guided the wheel. "I don't remember spending time with you like I did with Zeke."

Considering how Zeke turned out, maybe that's a good thing. I didn't say it.

Dad was sort of zoned out in memory. "We used to go to the park on Saturdays and I would take Zeke to the Children's Museum. By the time you came around, there was so much going on that there just didn't seem to be time."

My stomach growled and my legs looked forward to burning as I got to hold the pizzas on the way home.

***

Grey met up with me in the hallway by my locker. "Hey," she said. "Got a favor to ask."

"Yeah?"

"Ask Ms. Cohn, at your tutoring session tonight...."

I felt myself pale. "Yeah?"

"...if God is with us today."

I stared at her.

"And," she continued, "how we can get a hold of the *entire* book—the Old Testament. We don't call it that. What do we call it?"

I looked at her in blank ignorance.

"Exactly. I was looking through a Bible in the library here, and...."

I cut her off. "We have Bibles in the school library?"

"Yup."

"Isn't that against separation of church and state?" I asked.

A pimple-plagued, dirty-haired boy from sixth period English class came up and wanted to get into his locker, which was next to mine. Grey didn't even look at his slimy hair or ripped jeans as she stepped out of his way.

She said, "They're here and they go from Genesis to Deuteronomy and then the Old Testament goes all the way to a book called Malachi."

I was looking at her with my eyebrows squinted and my forehead furrowed. My locker was open and spewing papers and books. My L.L. Bean orange bookbag was on the floor trying to catch what my locker was vomiting.

"You looked at a Bible?"

"Yeah. And you wouldn't believe how many psalms are in our prayer book. We just stole the words of David and stuck them, willy-nilly, into *The Gates of Prayer*."

The Gates of Prayer is our synagogue's prayer book, with gold writing on the blue cover and a little pink ribbon as a place marker. The prayer book is used in every Friday night and Saturday morning service. They open backwards.

At services, we sang in Hebrew and said things like, *Hear O' Israel, the Lord is our God, the Lord is one. Blessed is His glorious kingdom forever and ever,* and we had no idea where that statement came from, but it was in front of us in the prayer book, so we said it twice, if not more, every Sabbath.

I stared at Grey for a moment, her words were sinking in. By now most of the hallway was cleared. Poppy was bending down, shoving books into her bookbag, and where she was bending, her black wool skirt bunched out in a little "v" in the back. The same skirt she was wearing when she got slapped by that guy who then shoved Matters into the locker.

"Wait a minute," I said.

Grey gave me her inquisitive expression. One eyebrow arched.

Just then Merriman came around the corner. I ignored him and said to Grey, "You mean to tell me, when I get all of those books at my Bar Mitzvah, not *one* of them is the entire ...whatever we call it? Not one of them has the whole complete thing?"

"Nope," Grey said shaking her head.

"Then why am I doing this?" I yelled pushing away from my locker.

Poppy looked over at us as Grey, alarmed, said, "Doing what?"

Merriman watched me with intense curiosity. He swept his hair out of his eyes as though he wanted a clearer view of my meltdown.

"I'm having my Bar Mitzvah to get answers." I spewed, "To get knowledge about this God I keep hearing about, the God of Abraham and Isaac and Jacob. But nobody is giving me anything!"

Poppy slammed her locker and walked over, her bookbag zipped and slung over one shoulder, which she never does because she always says it will give her a bad back one day. Her voice rang in my head, "We need to be even for good posture."

The bookbag strap had grabbed her sweater and pulled it tight across her chest and the buttons that held it together were strained, revealing the pink of her bra. I worked really hard not to stare at that pink, that cotton candy....

Grey. Look at Grey.

Poppy thumped her bookbag down and listened. Merriman

had taken off his backpack, opened it by loosening the drawstring and reached in. Out of its gaping mouth, Merriman pulled out a scuffed black leather covered book.

"Here," he said.

Grey, Poppy and I looked at him.

"It's the whole thing," he said. "Read what you want."

Grey took it, flipped through the thin pages and then tried to hand it back.

Merriman shook his head, "Take it."

The hallway was empty now and all of the buses were gone. The only sounds were a radio coming from an art room a couple of doors away and an occasional scream from the cheerleaders as they ran the hallways in their practices.

"This is yours," Grey said. "It has your name in it and everything."

"And there are notes in the margins," Merriman said. "Take it."

Grey and Merriman locked eyes, continuing their argument in silence until Grey broke away, looking down—surrendered— and blushed. She glanced up again and said, trying hard not to smile, "You're not going to give up."

"Nope," Merriman replied. "Enjoy it."

The moment was serious. Poppy stood staring. I wasn't sure if she got it. Merriman was staring at Grey as her eyes were fixed to the book as she flipped through it. Her facial expression was hard to read. She was biting her lower lip and she was frowning, but she was holding the book almost like she was petting it.

"I'm sorry; I mean—" Poppy stammered, awkward like she'd walked in on them kissing. "I completely missed the bus."

"Don't worry about it," Merriman said. "You're coming with us."

***

We started at Starbucks, but then wound up at a pool hall, where I learned there are some things that Merriman really stinks at. Pool is one of them.

Poppy looked at Grey across the pool table and said, "So, you had a Bat Mitzvah?"

"Sure."

"What was it like?"

We all stopped for a second to listen, and then Merriman started to line up a shot.

"It was okay. I was really nervous, and I was really glad when it was over."

Merriman hit the cue ball. It sailed across the table, missed the ball he was aiming for and sunk itself in the side pocket.

"Nice," Grey said as she removed the cue ball from the end and figured out where she wanted to place it. Merriman grunted in good-natured frustration.

"What do you think of the whole Bat Mitzvah now?" I asked; we'd never even talked about it before.

Grey placed the cue ball down where she wanted it. "I guess I don't…think about it." She lined herself up for the shot, took it, and scratched.

"Nice," Merriman said mocking her as she had him.

She scowled at him and leaned on her pool stick.

"Why don't you think about it?" Poppy said watching me as I took the cue ball out of the end, as Grey had, and studied the table.

"That day, and studying for that day, was never a part of me. It was a part of my family, a part of my culture, but not a part of me."

"So, where are you now?" Merriman asked.

Grey thought for some time as she watched me line up to sink the solid red ball. The cue ball hit it, and the red ball was sent sailing down the table, exactly where I didn't mean for it to go.

Merriman started to walk around the table, looking at angles and possible shots. He asked his question again. "Where are you now?"

"I'm thinking." And after waiting while Merriman took and made his shot, she said, "I guess I'm looking for what I believe."

"Wouldn't your family hate it if you decided to believe something they don't?" Poppy asked.

I looked over at Poppy as she spoke. Her hair was pulled back in a crazy ponytail of curls. Her cheeks were flushed and she was looking a little perplexed.

"I don't really think of this as having anything to do with them. It has to do with...." she trailed off; Merriman had missed his shot and it was Poppy's turn.

"It has to do with what?" Poppy said as she studied the table for her shot.

"It has to do with..." Grey said furrowing her brow and chewing on the side of her cheek, "...God and me. Nobody else."

***

Merriman, Poppy and Grey dropped me off at the Rabbi's house after we spent the afternoon together. "Mrs. Cohn," I said, as I ran my finger along the edge of the white kitchen table, my mind set on the bowl in the center; it was full of those silly little oranges that my mom calls clementines. My legs were bouncing and my stomach was churning so bad I thought I was either going to let out one of the most rancid belches I have ever set free—and it would be a real shame to waste that on the Rabbi's wife—or I was going to throw up all over the place. Mom gives me Tums at times like this. How do you ask the Rabbi's wife for Tums?

Instead, I asked, "If God was with the people of the Torah, where is He today?"

She thought for a second or two and said, "He was with Abraham, Isaac and Jacob, so He's with us, of course."

Of course. "How?" I asked.

Papers were spread out in front of her, my essay among them. There were also photocopies of people's Torah portions—basically Torah text—in black Xerox copies, opposed to the brown handwritten text that is on the actual scrolls.

Mrs. Cohn was thinking; I was staring at the papers. Finally, she said, "God promised us in Deuteronomy that He would never leave us nor forsake us. So, He's here with us."

"Moses talked with God. As did Noah. And Joseph was given the gift of dream interpretation and he was blessed by God. How come we don't hear God today?"

"Maybe," Mrs. Cohn said, "we're not listening."

"Do you hear God?" I asked her without thinking before blurting the words out of my mouth. I really need to work on that.

She shook her head no. It was a slow movement, like a pendulum on a grandfather clock.

"How does one hear Him?" I asked.

"By listening."

"But you don't hear Him," I said. "Are you not listening?"

"The Jews are God's Chosen people. God will reveal Himself to us in His time."

"What will that look like?"

"Peace will reign in Jerusalem and Israel." Her eyes were bright. She was smiling, looking hopeful.

"Is that possible?" I was thinking of Channel One News that came on the T.V. mounted on the wall, near the ceiling in my homeroom every morning. This morning another one of the peace talks in Israel was on hold because the Israelites had entered Palestinian territory with tanks. All I remembered from the film clip was dark men in Nazi olive green, holding machine guns and running down a dirt road.

"Anything is possible with God," she said in her matter-of-fact way.

My mind was racing. I couldn't get a grip on her last statement. My thoughts reeled and slammed home on a single fear: "Mrs. Cohn, how do we know for certain we haven't missed it?"

She stared at me and I felt like my brain was being scanned like they do on Star Trek or something. "Look at the Jews today," she said. "They are still being blessed."

I wanted to ask how the holocaust was a blessing but I had enough sense (however little it was) to keep my mouth shut on that one.

"Shall we get to work?" she asked, holding out a copy of my Torah portion to me.

"Sure." I struggled through the words having to be corrected every third pronunciation.

***

I walked into the study late on Wednesday night. It had been a half-day at school because the next day was

Thanksgiving. I had not even realized it was coming up until, on Monday, when Mrs. Alberta was all, "I want to give you a test before you go away to eat all that turkey."

Zeke was in the study, much to my shock, grouching at the computer screen. "You know how to get the damn cursor over here?" he asked while tapping the screen. "I can't seem to get it to do what I want."

"Have you used the mouse?"

"Yeah, but the pad's messed up or something. The thing is ancient."

I looked at the cloth pad with its tropical underwater scene and orange clown fish, which had seen its set of Coke spills and was worn smooth. "Have you tried the TAB key?"

"No, I already have a soda," he said with his usual weasely sarcasm.

"Ha-Ha." I reached over to the keyboard and hit the TAB key at the top left. The highlighted section moved to where Zeke wanted to be.

"Thanks," he said. "Maybe you're not so bad."

"Uh, thanks," I muttered and stared at the form on the screen. "What ya' doin'?"

"On-line application for colleges."

"Isn't the deadline soon?"

Zeke shook his head. "Not for a couple of weeks. It is only the end of November."

The glow of the computer screen made his eyes have white squares in them.

"Don't remind me," I said. "My Bar Mitzvah is only three months away."

"Count down to B.M." He then grinned and said, "You know what B.M. stands for in nursing terms?"

"Big Mouth?"

"Bowel Movement. Think about *that* as you face the congregation from the bema to read the Torah."

"Zeke, if you weren't being so nice right now, I would say something rude."

"Just scared of pissing me off." He started to punch keys with his two index fingers.

"Maybe," I said, "but I won't miss you next year."

"Maybe I'll stick around just to torment you." He leaned into the computer screen to read.

"Not possible. I'm blessed by God. I'm His Chosen One. You will go away."

"Here's hoping," he said lifting his Coke can and took a sip.

"Amen!" I went to leave.

He stopped me dead in the doorway with a single question: "Haven't seen Yaba for a while; where is that security blanket?"

"Safe," I replied and ducked out fast.

***

Thanksgiving was filled with turkey, Mom barking orders, cranberry sauce, Mom barking orders, sweet potatoes with marshmallows on top and Mom barking orders. The entire family went into a food coma after the meal. Mom and Dad were in the two recliners; Grey was crashed on the comfy chair in the study; Zeke was locked up in his room and I had the family room couch. Snores could be heard all over the house. Of course, Grey didn't snore; she just sort of puffed air.

Black Friday, the day after Thanksgiving was the worst shopping day of the year, and Mom wanted to take Grey. They were *discussing* it in the kitchen. "I don't want to go," Grey yelled.

"I asked you last week," Mom replied, calmer but just as loud.

"I told Merriman that I would hang out with him. Dad said it was fine."

I thought Mom was going to force Grey into the car and handcuff her to the handle on the ceiling that Zeke loved to call, "The Oh-Shit Grip," when Merriman pulled up in his bright red Jeep. I watched from the living room. Merriman came to the front door; he smiled a smile I could only dream of having. It was cool and slick, and somehow, made him seem huge. He rang the bell.

I ran to the front door to let him in. I slid on the hardwood foyer floor in my white socks with a hole over the big toe. Grey came running to the door after I opened it.

He gave me a hey and then turned to her. "How about the

best treat ever?"

Mom, following Grey to the foyer, frowned. Grey's face matched Merriman's excitement.

"What? Where are we going?" Grey asked.

"Come with me and I'll show you."

Grey looked to Mom. Mom looked hard at Merriman and then, slowly, Merriman looked away from Grey to my Mom. "Mrs. Mariner, you don't mind me stealing Grey for a little while, do you?"

Mom frowned.

"Please Mom."

"We had plans," Mom said.

"Oh," Merriman said to Mom, "That's fine. We can do this some other time, Grey."

"Please, Mom," Grey pleaded. "You go to the mall, have a good time. I'll be fine."

"It's not you I'm worried about." She fixed her eyes on Merriman and said, "I don't like Grey going where I can't get in touch with her."

Merriman looked all serious for a moment or two. "I know, Ma'am. I got my Father's cell phone. He and my mother are out together so they have her phone and I got my Dad's. If it's okay for me to take Grey, I'll give you the number."

Mom stared even harder at Grey.

Grey said, "I hate shopping. You know this. I'm only going to make you miserable. Why force me?"

"You need clothes," Mom said.

Grey looked at her like she was nuts. "Not really. What I have is fine."

Mom sighed and said, "Fine. Go. Enjoy."

Grey squeeked with delight and rushed out the door. Merriman hung back to leave Mom with the cell phone number. Mom was still frowning down at the piece of paper in her hand when the Jeep pulled out of the driveway. Grey got freedom that day and I was dragged around the mall.

***

That night I dreamt of my future wife.

My future wife will be a thin, rugged, muscle woman who loves a pack on her back, hiking boots on her feet. She will play with bugs and skinny-dip. Her hair will be golden rain that licks my body leaving it shivering. Her nails will leave streaks on my back and all of her will embrace me as I sweat for her.

I fear I will soil her, dirty her when I explode, *but* she will be *my* wife.

***

Back in school on Monday, I started out with Algebra. Mrs. Alberta was standing in the front "teaching." Letters are meant for words, not numbers. Whoever thought this up, this variable stuff, was doing some serious illegal drugs.

"Whatever you do to one side, you do the same to the other," she said. "Now, who would like to explain why?" Her hair was pulled back in a tight bun and her forehead was becoming larger and larger from the years of being tugged back with such determination. The hair follicles were giving in and falling out. Maybe one day she would wind up with hair like a Sumo wrestler. Just gray instead of black.

"Alex," she said. "Why don't you come up here and explain why this works."

"No thank you."

"Alex, I've asked you to come."

"I thanked you for the opportunity. I really do appreciate it."

"Alex, this is no longer a request. Come on up and demonstrate this."

I pulled my slug body out of the seat and trudged up to the white board. I took the dry erase marker with its brain cell killing fumes and faced the board. My feet began to sweat and my hands shook. The marker squeaked across the board as I demonstrated how to find the area of a triangle and why it needs to be $1/2b(h)$.

Mrs. Alberta turned, pounced on the marker and sent me back to my seat, roaring, "Alex, this is Algebra, not Geometry." For the rest of the class, she burrowed a hole in my forehead with her cat's eyes, which was—thankfully—only another 15 minutes.

***

As class ended, Poppy grabbed her books and made a beeline out the door. I fumbled with my books and rushed after her leaving Matters to find his next class on his own.

"Really, Alex, you need to learn to control yourself," Poppy said harshly as we walked down the downstairs hallway of the school. The trees and walkways of freedom were just outside the big windows next to us. Bright light poured through them, light that most classrooms didn't get even get a hint of. The architects must have thought dark gloomy fluorescent chambers would be best for students' attention spans and learning styles.

"I have complete control. I just wanted to liven things up."

She made a *tutt* sound and started to walk faster. Her hips would have been swiveling like mad—if I could have seen them under the huge forest green sweatshirt she "borrowed" from her brother.

"Where the rush to?" I asked.

"Not to. From."

"From?"

"You," she said stopping short.

I had been careening forward to keep up with her and tried to stop when she did. I wound up tripping over my feet and almost dropped all of my books.

"What?" I asked.

"You piss me off," she hissed.

I stood up and looked at her. Her eyebrows were furrowed in V's and a large crease had formed in the center of her forehead just above her nose. Her lips, light pink and tempting, were slammed shut. My stomach sunk as I realized we were in the middle of another fight.

"What did I do wrong?"

"You breathe!"

I looked to the left, windows. The right, lockers and doorways to classrooms. Teachers I didn't know, in suits and pink-flowered dresses, were peaking their heads around doorways to look out at us. Students in backpacks and ripped sneakers were scuffing to slow down in order to eavesdrop.

"Yeah, so what if I don't get Algebra? Okay, so I'm not as smart as you. That's what bothers you?"

"No," she snapped. "It's that you don't mind pretending to be a fool."

"I don't pretend to be a fool," I yelled. "I am a fool."

A couple of cute girls in short skirts standing along the wall snorted.

I didn't know Poppy's face could do those weird things: lip up on one side, eyes like Miss Piggy when she's about to attack.

"I mind very much. You, Mr. Fool Mariner, can find a new best-friend. Go find Matters. I'm sick of this. I'm sick of how I get dragged down because you're not afraid to look stupid." She hurried away and I watched her disappear around the corner.

***

"Well," Zeke drawled as he walked into the family room just as my favorite rerun came on. "I hear you've got a girlfriend."

"Nope," I said not looking up.

"That's not what I hear."

"What have you heard?"

"Is she putting up a fight?"

"I'm not talking about this with you," I mumbled.

"What will she say about the fact you still have a security blanket?" Zeke was jumping around in front of the couch all excited.

"Nothing, she'll never find out."

"Not if I tell her."

"Listen," I said, not taking his bait, "If you want to jump around like an idiot that's fine. You're just in the way of the T.V."

"Don't you want to talk about this?"

"Not with you," I said trying to see around his fat butt.

"With Grey?"

"I don't know. But you are not on my list."

Zeke flopped down on the couch and looked at me. "Why not?"

"We don't get along. You know that. You're not going to

spill out all of your wet fantasies about Michelle to me. Why would I talk to you about Poppy?"

"What if I did talk to you about Michelle?" Zeke asked.

"I'd think you'd been hitting some pretty powerful drugs and would tell Mom and Dad to have you tested." I refused to look at him. I was staring hard at the T.V. trying hard to follow the conversations between Mr. and Mrs. Seaver, the T.V. parents who always did everything right.

He snorted, but then got quiet. "You know what?"

I didn't say anything, but continued to stare ahead of me.

"I'm sorry," he said.

I swung my head around fast to look at him. At first, I thought he was joking, but he had this weird expression on his face. His eyes were on the carpet and he was frowning like he was thinking about what he was saying. If I hadn't been slouching down, already seated on the couch, I would have fainted. All of my blood was pooled; there was no place for me to fall.

"I've been real mean and ...."

I sat up fast and threw the remote at him. "Here. Take it if you want it. Don't act all nicey, nicey like this. It wigs me out. If you want something, just beat me up for it. I understand that."

Zeke looked at the remote and then looked at me. "I don't want the remote. I wanted to say I'm sorry."

I stared at him no longer aware of the T.V., or that Grey was standing in the doorway or the fact that I was really wanting to be down at Poppy's house working out peace after our scene in the hallway.

"What do you want, Zeke?"

He didn't say anything for a moment or two then he said. "I don't want to be Hitler. I don't want you to hate me. I really wanted you to like me, and I thought that other stuff was a way to do it."

I stared and wanted to say, *Oh, yeah, real endearing*, but truth was, I ached to hear the rest of what he had to say.

"Goss, my best-friend, has decided to abandon me and is going to some school in Michigan."

"I heard."

"And you're my little brother," he said looking over. "I

should be helping you and not beating you up."

"I give you a hard time," I said.

"Deserved. I've deserved every hard time you've given me."

"This has been the strangest day," I said.

Just then Zeke busted out in this crazy insane laughter. "Ha! You bought that! Ha-Ha! You're an even bigger loser than I thought! HA!" He lunged.

I was off guard and was flung from the couch smushed to the beige fuzzy carpet in one swift action. I just laid there, pressed under Zeke, wind knocked out of me, pinned, not at all clear on what had just occurred. Grey left the doorway; I was forced to find air and freedom on my own.

***

I had been practicing, a little. I had big plans to show off what I'd remembered.

"Bar-uch a-tah A-do-nai, El-o-hay-nue, Mel-ech Ha-o-lam," I said to Mrs. Cohn.

"Good," she said when I finished. "I think we're going to be all set when the big day comes."

"It's not for like two and half months," I said.

"Exactly," she replied. "We're going to spend a lot of that on your Torah portion."

"I almost know it," I lied.

She frowned and said nothing as she shuffled papers on the white table. All of a sudden she looked up at me, her face sharp with anger, her gaze locked on me. "Where do these questions about God come from?"

"Myself," I said, a little startled. "And Grey, but they make sense."

"Would you have thought these things without her asking these questions?"

"Sure. They make sense."

"Right," she said. "So let's get started."

***

I dreamt of the ocean last night. All cool and big. I dreamt of a shark circling around the bottom. Circling for weeks, almost a month. Circling down in the depths. About 5 feet from the bottom. The bottom about 30 feet down. Circling. Circling. Circling and then. I was swimming. Swimming with fingers extended pushing thick water. Moving the water out of the way in the breaststroke, pushing, kicking like a frog. A frog in saltwater. I swam. The shark circled. I swam. He circled. I swam. He charged and I was no longer swimming. I felt no pain. I was no longer anything, just crimson in the dense blue water.

***

The day after my shark dream, I approached Poppy in the cafeteria. She was sitting with a group of friends separated from our normal little clique. Matters was across the room eating with some of the math geeks he loved to hang out with.

"Can I sit here?" I asked as I put my brown lunch bag on the table.

"Whatever."

All the other girls at the table smiled at me. Ignoring them, I sat down next to her. I opened my lunch, took a bite of my sandwich and chewed. She did the same. We were silent while the other girls started to talk about cheerleading and lip gloss. I wasn't paying attention.

"You still mad?" I asked.

She said, "I don't get you, Alex."

The girls stopped to listen. I spoke anyway, "How's that?"

"Everybody knows that I've been tutoring you in Alegbra. You understand it, or you seem to when you leave my house. Then when you're asked to do exactly what we've gone over, you act like some big dufus."

I was silent and continued to chew my bologna, cheese and mustard sandwich.

"Why is that?"

I could feel her eyes on me. I still couldn't look at her. I swallowed, took a sip of my fruit punch and said, "I am a dufus?"

"No. You're not."

After another long silence that made me want to get up and leave, she said, "You just act like it."

I started to laugh and coughed hard because I choked on the Dorito I had just put in my mouth.

"You okay?" she asked, all concerned.

I continued to cough up my lung. Then, I took a sip of fruit punch and said, "I get nervous and can't stop myself."

She started to laugh this insane laugh that I had only heard a couple of times in our friendship.

"What?" I asked.

When she could breathe again, she said, "I got an image of what a dufus you're going to be at your Bar Mitzvah."

"Gee, thanks," I said as I shoved the last of my sandwich into my mouth. Through chews and smushed bread I mumbled, "I hope not."

***

Hannukah came and went. I got Poppy flowers. Mom and Dad asked me what she gave me, I said, "Oh, she promised to take me to the movies. And to make me dinner one night. And to teach me Algebra."

Dad laughed, "If she can do that, I will call her a saint."

"I thought we don't believe in them," I said.

Merriman had given me a book I couldn't read until after the Bar Mitzvah. I showed Grey when she stopped by to say that she and Merriman were going to a town hockey game and that she wanted to borrow my Fliers jersey. Her eyes were wide as I held out the hard covered book that read "Life Application Bible" on it. She said, "Hide it," as she handed it back to me.

Funny, you would think I was hiding a gun, drugs, something really awful. I was hiding a Bible in a Jewish home.

***

Weeks passed and B-M Day moved closer. Zeke kept calling it "Bowel Movement," and Mom hit him every time.

"I will say," she said once. "I can't wait until this is over and then we can stop going to synagogue."

"What?" I asked.

"What will be the point?" she said. "Your father and I don't really like it. It's for you that we go."

My jaw hit the ground. My brain whirred like a fan and then began to click like someone had put a playing card in the fan's blades. Why were they making me do this, if they didn't like it? Why was I going through all of this so they could just leave the synagogue after I was done? It clicked, at some very low-lying level that being Jewish doesn't matter. It doesn't matter what religion you are. Maybe God didn't matter either....

"You don't like it?" my mouth asked without my brain's connecting the words.

"Oh, Alex. Don't look so surprised. You've known that." She spoke like she did after making a big meal for fifteen people and was faced with a kitchen of dirty dishes.

I looked at her and wanted to say, *You know, I've been thinking about Christianity*, but I kept my mouth shut.

"I will also be excited to not have to pay all of this money. We have a hall, a D.J., catering and the invitations out. Aren't they great?" She reached over to the counter by the phone in the kitchen and showed me an invitation, like it was the first time I had seen them. A white card with navy blue outlining, it had a navy blue and silver Jewish Star of David in the top right. The writing was all navy blue. She had picked them out.

"Great." I sighed.

"Come on, Alex. You said so yourself. There was nothing else that you really liked."

"Right, but I didn't want *you* to pick them out for me."

"What would you have picked?"

"Probably those," I admitted.

"Then don't say anything else about it."

I shut my mouth and left the room.

***

I needed a suit for the Bowel Movement. I wanted to take Merriman along. He would know cool. Mom didn't like me going without her. I brought up the invitations and all of a sudden she was like, "Fine go. You can look with him, but I won't let you buy anything without me."

After a bouncing ride in the red Jeep with Sonic Flood pumping from the speakers, Merriman took me to Macy's and then to Lord and Taylor. We agreed they were Mom's kind of stores. We went to Bacharach. It had rich wooden floors and funky colors all over the place. There were shirts in stacks on the walls, but they didn't have any of that plastic wrapping. There were ties in fountains on the tables and the shoes, all leather, smelled better than any of my shoes ever smelled. Of course, it was a men's store, but we found, after much joking, that I was bigger than I had believed. I always saw myself as the equivalent of a 12-year old wimp.

"Must be all that wrestling with Zeke," Merriman said as he brought me a tie. It was silver and blue and shimmered in diamond shapes. It looked just like what Mom would want me to be wearing.

"Did I tell you Zeke has been pulling these elaborate apologies and then he pummels me when I'm about to forgive him?"

"That boy should get some help."

We decided that black pants and a black sleek jacket with the shimmer tie was the way to go. I would just need to convince my mother that she should spend about as much as it would cost for the D.J. on my outfit.

"But you look cool," Merriman said. "Even if your mother doesn't allow you to get this, know that there will be a time in the future when you will look fantastic."

***

Mom sat me down in the kitchen the day after shopping with Merriman. I told her all about what we found. She admitted it sounded *cool*, except for the price.

The little lampshaded chandelier was glowing down on us. The lights were reflected in the polished wood of the kitchen table. The windows revealed a gray sky and the thought of snow. Mom said, "I will get you the cool outfit on one condition."

"What's that?" I asked sitting forward a little.

"You study." She waved away my attempt at an argument.

"Mrs. Cohn has called me on a number of occasions saying she has concerns about your not being ready. That you haven't been taking your Torah portion seriously and that you need to do more work on it."

"I don't even know what I'm saying. How am I supposed to take it seriously?"

"Alex, there comes a time that you just need to do stuff you don't like."

"Then why aren't you going to synagogue after I'm done?" I demanded.

"Because I've done it for forty-three years. You only need to work for three more months. Can you handle that?"

"But then, when it's over, do I get to do what I want?"

Mom frowned. "I don't know. You are only almost 13. What are we talking about?"

I didn't say anything.

She looked at me with her eyebrows raised but said, "Then I can't answer you."

I wanted to open my mouth and spill it all. I wanted to tell her about Grey's thoughts about Christianity, about a God who could love her and know her personally. A lump came up in my throat. I didn't know why.

***

Merriman, Grey and I all went out to ice cream at Friendly's early on Saturday, before Merriman had plans to take Grey to the city for a Valentine's Day thing. She didn't know where they were headed and Merriman whispered the plans to me when Grey got up to go to the bathroom.

We were all sharing a five-scoop Reese's Pieces sundae. The thing was massive, but not as massive as I remembered them being when I was little. The marshmallow and peanut butter sauce licked the back of my throat in warmth while the vanilla ice cream cooled my brain and almost gave me one of those raging headaches from eating too fast.

"Winter is the best time to eat ice cream," Grey said when she got back from the bathroom and picked up the spoon she had left in the "glass" to try to stop us from eating too much while she was gone.

"Hear! Hear!" Merriman said.

I agreed, "But I don't know why."

Grey laughed. "Because Silly, you can eat as much as you want, gain a couple of pounds and nobody is ever going to notice."

"And," Merriman said, "those pounds help keep you warm when you are snowboarding."

Grey was sitting next to Merriman and they were both facing me. Grey's hair fell down into her eyes and she blew it out of the way. When she would get really frustrated with it, she would wipe her hands off on her napkin and then tuck it behind her ear. All of our spoons were sticky with ice cream because we kept fighting each other for the good stuff. I got a whole glop of peanut butter and marshmallow and Merriman, with a squeak, took his spoon, scraped mine and stole it all. Before I could even utter a syllable, he had it in his mouth with a gleam in his eye. This was war.

We would fight each other's spoons and try to sneak mouthfuls while the others were distracted. Somehow it all got eaten and very little was dripped onto the pale green table. We all left the cherry for Grey. She grinned as she put the whole thing, stem too, in her mouth.

Merriman and I stared at her and she said, "Watch."

We waited some time, and started to talk about my studying for my Bar Mitzvah.

"So," he said, "what does having a Bar Mitzvah do for you?"

"I'm considered an adult."

"What does that mean?" Merriman said.

"Um, I get to stop going to Hebrew school."

"That's it?"

I looked to Grey. She was still busy with the cherry stem in her mouth. She kept moving her mouth in funny ways, almost like a cow chewing its cud. She shook her head and stuck one finger up in the air: *Wait*.

"What does this mean to God?" he asked.

"It's, um...." I hadn't thought about this before.

"I don't know," I said after some time.

Merriman said, "I know how that is. I've done stuff and haven't thought about what God thinks. It's been stupid stuff though, not something as important as a Bar Mitzvah."

Just then Grey gave a little jump in her seat, brought her hand up to her mouth and took the cherry stem out. She had tied it in a knot with her tongue.

Merriman took it from her, all spit covered and said, "Now that's impressive. Anything else that tongue can do?"

Grey blushed. I don't think I've ever seen her blush before. I've seen her flush red from anger, but never blush.

I watched as she reached over and took the knotted stem from him. "Really," she said, "and you call yourself a good Christian boy."

"I call myself a Christian," Merriman said, "but I never said I was perfect."

Grey laughed and I took the last spoonful of ice cream.

***

Over the table at the Cohn's house, I began to read my Torah portion. The Rabbi was upstairs. I thought he could hear every flaw I made, judging me and knowing I wouldn't be ready in time. My fear was that he would see what evil thoughts I had lurking in the back, dark rooms of my brain and say I would never make a good Jew.

As it was, as I was reading the Torah portion, Mrs. Cohn had to stop me only three times to make me go over something again, correcting my pronunciation.

As I was leaving, standing in the doorway, Mrs. Cohn was standing next to me. I said, "Can you call my mom and tell her? I would like to be able to go and get my outfit soon."

She smiled and said, "I was planning on calling her and telling her without your even asking."

"Thanks," I said, but my smile faded fast. I grunted a good-bye and turned and headed down the walk. I felt my eyebrows furrow. I made my feet move fast.

She saw the change in me before I turned my back. She saw my face fall and looked concerned as I ran away. I gave her a quick wave and a fake smile as I got into Dad's black Ford

Expedition. He wanted to know all about how it went. Only I didn't want to talk. I wanted to say nothing. My legs began to shake, and my throat seized up. My tongue began to sweat and my armpits grew hair at an insane rate.

If Mrs. Cohn had called Mom to give her updates on my progress, what's to have stopped her talking about the questions I was asking about Jesus? I mean, it would be a concern for any Jewish person to have their child asking questions about Jesus. And asking the Rabbi's wife is a pretty stupid thing to be doing. They weren't all my questions; some were Grey's. But she's not the one studying like some stupid robot who doesn't think for himself but just does what he's told. All because of one day that means so much for *everybody* else. All Grey has to do at my Bar Mitzvah is say one line of Hebrew. She's already got it down. Go her. The spotlight will be on me; Alex. I can just hear the Rabbi at *my* Bar Mitzvah. He will call me to the bema so that he can praise my efforts in becoming a Bar Mitzvah. I can just hear what he's going to say.

"Alex," he'll say, his voice like cool water. "I've been watching you grow up. I've seen how you interact with your brother, Zeke; how you treat each other. You know, you only have your family. You need to learn to care for and appreciate each other.

"I've seen how you act with Grey," he'll continue. "You look out for her and try to protect her when she might be getting into trouble. You also do her grunt work and get pulled into her thinking. Don't let your family members distract you."

He'll tell me what wonderful and supportive parents I have and how I need to appreciate them. He'll say stuff I won't remember 15 minutes after it's over and we're all hanging out at the party. I'll just remember that it would have embarrassed me and made me feel like I didn't deserve any of the time *anyone* has ever spent talking to or trying to help me.

Dad interrupted my thoughts as we almost got to the driveway.

"You've been real quiet. Is everything okay?"

"I think so," I mumbled. Then said, "Is Grey home?"

"I think she's going to dinner with Merriman."

"He's got a funny name," I said.

"A little. But you like him," Dad said. "Right?"

"Yeah."

"So what's the matter?"

I didn't say anything.

Dad pulled into the driveway and into the open garage. I popped my seat belt while he was still parking. When he turned off the ignition, I yanked open the door and leapt out of the passenger seat. Dad called after me, but I ignored him as I ran up the beige stairs by the family room to find Grey in her bedroom. She was reading on her bed.

"You really should knock first," she said.

"Mom'sbeengettingcallsfromMrs.Cohn," I sputtered.

"What?" she said, sitting up a little.

"Mrs. Cohn has been calling Mom to talk to her about how I'm doing," I said a little slower.

"Yeah, so?"

"Don't you get it?"

Grey looked at me, thinking hard, but no lightbulbs were going on in her mind. She just sat there, head cocked and staring at me like I was nuts.

"I've been asking Mrs. Cohn questions about *Jesus*. What if she told Mom?"

Grey paled. The two of us stared at one another, neither knowing what to say.

After a couple of seconds, I flopped down on the white down comforter that covered her bed, "What do we do?"

Grey sat back, eyes on the ceiling. "Nothing for now."

"What?"

"Yeah. We wait. Let's watch them and see what they do."

"What do we do?" I repeated like I was my aunt's stupid parrot.

"What we have been doing," Grey replied. "Ask questions and make decisions for ourselves."

"What do you mean?" I asked leaning up on my elbow to look at her with my hand pressed against my cheek. My cheek was pulled to the side, up toward my ear.

She didn't look at me at first. She looked down at her book and then at the ceiling, but then she looked at me and said in a small voice, "I didn't want to tell you until after your Bar

Mitzvah...."

She took a long pause and then whispered, "I'm a Christian."

The world stopped.

After a long moment of silence while I let her words and what they really meant to seep in. I asked, "When?"

She didn't look at me as she spoke. She held her eyes on her hands in her lap and said, "A couple of weeks ago, the night we went out to Friendly's and Merriman and I went walking along the river in the city. We held hands and looked at the boathouses still all decorated in white lights. And then I asked him some tough questions. He was so patient and answered until I really understood. Then I asked what I needed to do. He prayed and then I knew what I was doing made sense. You with me?" she asked, looking up at me for the first time.

"I think."

She looked at me and smiled. "I know I shouldn't tell you, but it has changed how I look at myself and the world. I know that sounds trite, but I seem to care more about what's going on around me than I did before."

I wasn't sure I knew what trite meant. I wanted to say and ask so much. But, instead, I stood up and said, in a monotone, "Congratulations."

"Alex, don't be this way," she said. "Please. I need you to understand."

I started to the door.

"Wait," she called after me.

"Huh?" I asked over my shoulder.

"Tell me you understand."

I looked at her, on her bed, leaning forward, her green eyes searching me. They were turning glassy like she was about to cry.

"I do understand," I whispered, turning and looking at the pale blue carpet as far away from her as I could. I faced a window that looked out onto the backyard, which was covered with untouched snow.

Then, I turned and left.

***

Later that week, Mom and I went shopping. We went to Bacharach and got light khaki pants, a navy blue shirt and the blue and silver shimmery tie that Merriman and I picked out. I tried stuff on for Mom, a bunch of different colored pants, blue, black, and different shirts, even a purple one. Mom thought the different colors were fun to try. I really considered the purple, but realized the whole thing was being done in navy blue and I should match that. At least, that's what Mom said.

Mom asked me, "Why do you think Merriman doesn't have a nickname?"

"Good question," I replied. "Maybe he really likes to be odd."

"But going by Manny would be okay," she said.

"Mom," I said, "Merriman and Manny sound different. And if he went by Merry, that would be too much like, 'Merry Christmas'."

"True," Mom said. "Here, let me see what you look like in this," and she threw a lime green shirt at me.

"You have to be kidding."

"I am. But I would like to see just how bad it is."

What scared us both was, it wasn't that bad at all. We still decided to stick with the navy. When I put the lime green shirt back, I was smiling and humming a song I'd heard in Merriman's Jeep. When she paid for it all, my face paled. "Oh my," I whispered.

"Forget the price," she said as we were leaving the store. "This is a once-in-a-lifetime day and you need the best."

***

Mom and Dad went off to the study that night to chat. They took their cups of decaf and headed in with a comment to us: *be good.*

"Aren't we always?" Zeke asked as he went to watch T.V.

I snorted in reply. I was in the kitchen, sitting at the breakfast bar with my English assignment out in front of me. It would be easier to do it on the computer but one, the computer was in the study and Mom and Dad were in there. And two, my

English teacher is a freak who wants everything handwritten.

My head was bent over my work and I was drinking an IBC root beer out of the brown bottle that looked like a beer bottle. Grey came in and asked me, "Do you want some ice cream?" as she started to dish herself some.

"Yeah, but could you throw it in a glass for me?"

She gave me an odd smirk but did as I requested. I poured my root beer over the glass full of vanilla praline fudge ice cream.

"You are so weird." She laughed as she started to spoon her own ice cream into her mouth.

Zeke came in and frowned. "Where's mine?"

"Get it yourself," Grey said getting out of his way.

"No." Then he turned to me, "Alex, you get it for me."

"I'm doing my English right now."

"Little Boy, that's not the proper response," he said.

I kept my eyes focused on my English.

"Little Boy," he repeated.

"Leave him alone," Grey said.

"You stay out of this, if you don't want to get yourself hurt."

"Hey," I said looking up for the first time, "you will not threaten her."

"What?" He sounded shocked.

"You will not threaten her."

"Are you going to stop me, Pip-Squeak?"

"You are such a bastard," I said looking back down at my homework.

I heard him coming and didn't even try to move. Grey yelled for Zeke to stop, but he didn't. I felt him connect; I went flying off my stool and on the way down, slammed my chin down on the counter. I landed with a thud on the floor, my head ringing, my shoulder aching, and my chin throbbing.

"Mom! Dad!" Grey yelled as loud as she could and then she came over to us. "Zeke! Leave him alone! Don't Zeke!" I felt his foot make contact with my knee, then a few seconds later a ripple of pain shot out of my knee and exploded all through my leg.

I screamed out.

"Oh, he can take it. Can't you, Sport?" Zeke said to me holding out his hand like he was helping me up.

I curled up tighter. I refused his hand. "Go away."

"Oh my God!" I heard Mom say a couple of seconds later.

"What?" was all I heard Dad say.

I felt myself being lifted up in someone's arms. The thought of being that close to Zeke was just repulsive and so I started to fight and squirm. My shoulder was killing me, but I still managed to try to punch Zeke.

But then I heard Zeke say, "See, there's still kick in him." His voice came from way across the room.

Dad's chest rattled in my ear when he replied, "Go away and don't show your face out of your room."

"But Dad-"

"I said, Go!" Dad roared.

I heard Zeke begin to move away from us down to his bedroom near the study. Dad turned and headed up the stairs to my room with me still in his arms.

Before we were in the bedroom, a great lump rose in my throat and I tried to swallow, but it made me choke. I breathed in deeply and took in Dad's safe smell. I slammed my eyelids closed tighter than before, but that didn't stop the rush of tears from streaming down. My whole body began to shake and the more I tried to get the shaking to stop, the more it shook.

Dad opened the door to my bedroom and put me down on my bed.

"Where's Yaba?" he asked.

"Hiding," I stuttered.

"Do you want me to find him?"

I shook my head no. "It's okay," I said. I tried to pull my knees up to my face and smush my eyes into them to stop crying but pain soared up my leg as I did so. All I did was hurt.

"Tell me about what's been going on," Dad said sitting down on my bed.

With the floodgates of tears opened, I spilled it all. All that I had been putting up with at home when Mom and Dad were out. All that had happened in the hallways at school. Even that friend of Zeke's who shoved Matters in a locker. I told him everything. I even talked about how I was sometimes at fault. I never looked at him. I covered my eyes with my elbow and spoke through sobs.

Dad listened and asked questions like, "Where was Grey when all of this was going on?"

"There or hiding," I replied. "What could she do to stop it?"

"Tell us," Dad said.

"And then get attacked herself? I don't blame her for being silent."

"What happened tonight?" he asked.

"He wanted ice cream and demanded we get it for him. Grey said no; I said no. He started to pick on Grey so I stood up for her. Then, he kicked the stool out from under me."

Dad reached over and moved my arm down and turned my face to the bedside light. "You're going to have a nasty bruise there, come tomorrow."

"I could claim it was full-contact Bar Mitzvah tutoring."

"Or you could tell people the truth," he said.

I looked at him but stayed silent.

"Tell them your brother abuses you," he said.

And then, looking at my Dad at that moment, his face looked old. His shoulders were hunched and he seemed almost like my grandfather when he had gone into the hospital for kidney stones. Soon after, Dad left my room.

Mom came in with a bag of frozen peas to put on my chin and a mug of hot cocoa. She sat down and asked, "Do you want to talk?"

I shook my head.

"Don't worry about your homework. We're going to write you a note that will excuse you for one night."

I mumbled, "Thanks."

Then we were silent for a long time.

Eventually, Mom asked, "Do you want anything?"

"No," I said. The peas were on my chin and the cocoa helped to warm my face when I took a sip of it.

"I'm going to go talk to your father," she said. "If you need anything, give a call." She took the cocoa mug out of my hand and put it on the bedside table. She lowered the peas and put them next to the mug. She sat down next me and her warm arms wrapped around me in a tight hug. She said, "I love you very much, my little Alex."

I couldn't speak. That lump in my throat tightened and I tried to swallow, but it wouldn't go away. Coughing didn't make it leave either. Squeezing my eyes tight as I could and still they began to leak. I didn't want to let go.

***

The next morning, I woke with a start. My alarm hadn't gone off and my bedside table clock said it was 9:07. I tried to jump but my leg rang out in pain. I hobbled down the stairs. Mom was standing in the kitchen in blinding daylight.

"Good morning, Sunshine," she said to me as I limped in.

"Mom? Why am I not in school?" I asked but my words slurred.

"Come here," she said like she didn't hear me.

"What?" I asked approaching her. She cupped my face and turned me to the light. "Have you looked at yourself yet?"

"No," I said trying to pull away because her touching me made it hurt even more.

"Well, you don't look so good."

"I hurt," I said as I was released.

"How bad?"

"I don't know. I ache."

"I'm taking you to the doctor's today. We already have an appointment at 2:00," she said.

"Mom! Why?"

"Alex," she said putting up her hand. Her nostrils flared a little and her eyes got glassy. "Don't argue with me on this one." She turned to the refrigerator, but I still saw that she had begun to cry.

"Do you want eggs for breakfast?" she asked, her words trembling.

"Sure," I said and looked at the breakfast bar and where I had been sitting the night before. I remembered it all, slow-motion.

"Man," I said as I tested out each part of my body to find out what hurt. "He can be such a jerk."

Mom dropped an egg, and it smacked splattering white and

yoke on the kitchen floor. "I'm sorry," Mom said starting to cry harder as she bent down to clean it up.

I began to panic. "Mom, it's just an egg."

She chuckled or was it a sob? I couldn't tell. Her hands were up to her face and she was beginning to cry really hard.

"Mom," I said.

She wouldn't move. She just crouched there. Sobbing.

I grabbed her shoulder and tried to get her to move to a chair, saying, "Mom, come on. Sit down. It's okay. I'll make the eggs."

Dad came in. What was he doing home?

"Julie, go on upstairs. Shower. Relax. I'll make Alex his breakfast."

"No," she said looking up at him. Her face, especially around her eyes, was bright red. "Alex, I'm not sorry about the egg."

"Oh," I said not getting it.

"I'm sorry about what's been going on. I'm sorry he's been so mean. I'm sorry I didn't know to stop it. I didn't think it had gotten as bad as it had."

She began to bawl. Dad went over to her, lifted her arms, pulled her up from the floor and led up her upstairs. While they were gone, I cleaned up the broken egg. Bending down made my knee scream, my chin throb and my head ache.

Dad came back down and started to cook for me. We were both silent.

When Dad handed me a plate with scrambled eggs, toast and bacon, he said, "We've contacted a counselor and we're going to start sending Zeke."

"Oh," I said picking up the fork, numb and slow.

"We're going to talk to your pediatrician and see what he thinks about you attending counseling separately from him."

"Do I have to?"

"It could be good for you," Dad said.

I started to put food in my mouth. Carefully. Chewing was painful.

"Zeke is also going to get a job; he's not getting any more allowance, so anything he wants, he's going to have to buy it for himself."

I continued to eat and every-so-often snuck a glance at Dad. He still looked old, but not as old as last night.

"I have also told him that he will start to do community service. He gets to decide where, but I've warned his guidance counselor that he will be coming in to get information. If he doesn't have information or ideas when he gets home tonight, I'm going to choose something for him." Dad looked at me, "You okay?" His expression was serious.

I put a bit of toast in my mouth. Dad studied my face for a couple of seconds and then turned to the pan on the stove.

"Your Mom's okay," he said. "She just feels betrayed by Zeke. She can't trust him and she feels really protective of you. She'll be okay, just give her some time."

I continued to chew with slow, gentle bites.

***

I stayed home the rest of the week. Milked it for all I could. The doctor said I had no serious physical injuries. I saw the counselor, Bryce. I was going to be meeting with him at his office every Thursday for at least a while. He seemed cool. Dad said he guessed Bryce was about 25. Bryce asked me to play basketball with him, if I was up to it. I told him I sucked at sports. He laughed and said, "Then your time with me is going to really help your game."

We went out to the hoop in the back, where no cars were parked. We just played and he asked a couple of questions like where I go to school and what my favorite subject is. I was sure he was just waiting to pull out the big guns for later. Maybe he was waiting for me to start talking. Just spill my guts all at once.

Playing with him, despite my air balls, was cool. He was down to earth and funny. He told me some stories about his huge mess-ups on the court and before I knew it, our time was up. It seemed strange my parents were spending money for counseling when I was learning how to play basketball. They seemed happy with the situation, so I guessed it was okay.

***

On Saturday, I went over to Poppy's. She took one look at the purple and blue splotch that had overtaken my chin and shook her head.

"Does that hurt?" she asked.

"Not really." We were heading down the stairs to her rec room where we were going to watch T.V. together.

"Did he get in trouble?"

"Like you wouldn't believe."

***

At Bar Mitzvah tutoring the next week, Mrs. Cohn said, "Great job." Her lips were chapsticked and her eyes were covered in black eyeliner and mascara. "I can see being bribed has really improved your motivation." If she noticed the bruise, she didn't say anything. At this point, it was a bright, disgusting yellow.

"Yeah," I replied looking down at the paper of Hebrew in front of me. "You know, I almost have this thing memorized."

"Good," she said. "Only don't recite it when you're at the Torah, read it. That way you're sure not to mess up."

"Right," I said. "But nobody will know if I do."

"Except you, me and the Rabbi," she said.

The people who mattered.

My mouth opened and I asked, "Did you tell my mom what I've been asking you?" before I could scare myself out of it.

She sat back and looked at me. "I thought that's what might have upset you at the end of last week's time."

I looked at her. Her eyes were concerned, the Crow's-Feet, as Mom calls those lines that shoot out from the corners of older people's eyes, were creased and she chewed a little at the side of her mouth. If she kept that up, she was going to need to put on more Chapstick.

"Well," she said, measuring her words like medicine. "I did tell your mom that you'd been asking some pretty serious questions about other religions."

I waited for more.

"And your mom said that it could have had something to do with Grey's influence on you."

I looked at her but said nothing.

She met my stare when she said, "Your mom is concerned about all of you."

We sat in silence.

"Can I ask you another question?" I asked.

"Sure, Alex. You can talk to me."

"What happens to you when you die?"

She sat back and sighed a little. "Jews are given very little in their books about death. We believe in Sheol, which is an afterlife, but we don't know what it looks like or what it will be. God talks about it in the prophesies."

"What prophesies?"

"You know Isaiah, Jeremiah, Daniel. A little bit in the Psalms too."

"Can I get a copy of them?"

She shook her head. "Not until later."

"Can I go buy it?"

"Sure. It's the Tenakah," she said.

"Can I go to Barnes and Noble and get it?"

"I think you may be a little young still."

"I become an adult in three weeks. How can I be too young?"

"Don't get upset, Alex. You will be an adult in the eyes of Judaism. If you really want to know this stuff, you can take the confirmation class next year."

That wasn't the information I was looking for. I've heard stories about the confirmation class. I've heard how they're more into eating candy and drinking soda than talking about God. They don't even have a book for that class. Not one of them has a Tenakah, or whatever she called it.

"You can take confirmation class next year," I mocked in a whiny voice as I stood on the front step waiting for Mom's green Volkswagon Golf to pull up.

***

I skulked through the living room and the kitchen and then headed outside to take a walk in the snow before it all changed from crunchy snow that swallowed my footsteps to melting ice.

I yanked the back door open. "Where you going?" Zeke called gruffly from his spot on the couch in the family room.

"Out," I replied.

"Check the mail for me when you come back in."

"Sure."

"Thanks."

I looked over my shoulder to see if it really was Zeke saying thank you. To my surprise, it was. The cold air filled my lungs and made my eyes sting. I squinted and started to tromp through the snow. The sky was bright blue and the sparkles on the snow were blinding. I headed across the side field, cut through a couple of the neighbors' property and headed for the woods. It was one o'clock. My nose was already starting to run. If I stayed out too long, there would be snot all down the front of my coat. I took my glove and swiped it across my face, making a yellow streak that turned white and then clear and froze.

Nothing and everything was on my mind.

What was going on in the house was at the front my mind. Mom was beginning to mellow out. Grey was out a lot with Merriman. It was like she was hiding or running away. I wished I could get out as much as she did, but there wasn't much freedom for me. Even on a Saturday like today.

When I did try to talk to Grey, she would say things like, "You gave me the chance to help out, and I wimped out on you." Or "I never stood up for you out of fear. That night you stood up for me and got pounded." I tried to tell her to relax and forget about it. But she couldn't seem to shake it.

Then there was Poppy. She and I had taken to sitting closer together when we watched movies in her family room. Her hair always smelled of bouquets of flowers and her eyes always shone when I looked deep into them. She was like this statue in a museum, that's so fantastic to be near, but I still couldn't touch it. My body ached in a way I never knew before.

When I talked to Grey about this, she said I was one of the most mature twelve year old she'd ever met. Truth was, what if I hurt Poppy? She was the most amazing thing I had ever had in my life. What if I broke her heart? What if I let her down? I would hate to see her cry. It would make me want to rip my heart out and hand it to her.

I trudged through the snow in the woods, stomping it down as I planted my foot with each new step. The cold air came into my lungs and out in a puff of fog. This cold around me didn't change how warm it made me to think about Poppy.

***

In school the following Monday, field-hockey captain Michelle caught up with me. She was wearing this totally hot shirt that came down to just above her full chest. It was pink and tight. It was hard to pay attention to her words.

Matters and I were talking outside my science class.

"Little Mariner," Michelle the Cheetah said.

When Matters saw her trying to catch up with me, he said, "Later," and moved off to his next class. Poppy shot us this really nasty glance as she headed down the hallway in the opposite direction toward Family and Consumer Science, a fancy term for Home Economics.

When she reached me, she said, "I'm hiding from Zeke."

I asked Michelle, "Why don't you want Zeke around?"

She really didn't give me a reason. She said that she was getting tired of his following her around. "But," she said with this sly grin, "I've got some stuff planned to make him change his mind about me."

Looking at her in her tight shirt and small black skirt and amazing tall and muscular legs, I didn't see how she was going to turn Zeke off.

"But you're graduating soon, and going away to college, so why not just wait it out?" I asked.

"I don't know."

"Who do you want to be with?" I asked.

Her pink lip-glossed lips formed a small smile, but she didn't say who.

"I could talk to them," I suggested.

Michelle flipped her beautiful blond ponytail and said, "You know, there is someone I'm thinking of, but I think he kind of has his eye on someone else."

"Who?" I asked.

"It looks like it might be working out between them."

"Who?" I asked.

"Merriman," she said looking at me.

I jumped back a little and bumped into the deep orange lockers behind me. She raised her eyebrows and a little bit of pink came up into her cheeks that matched her lip gloss.

Okay, so if there was one person Michelle couldn't compete with, it was Grey.

"So, they are pretty serious aren't they?" she asked.

"I think so, but I could still talk to Merriman about you and see what he thinks."

She snorted. "I don't think it will do much good, but thanks." She leaned over and kissed me on the cheek. The spot where her lips touched me burned and I felt a hot rush enter that spot, soar down my neck, flood my chest and made my toes curl up inside my once-white-now-gray Nike sneakers. The familiar ache inside formed so fast as I watched her wiggle down the hall away from me.

***

Merriman had made arrangements to pick me up after tutoring on Tuesday at the Cohn's house. The ride over to Starbucks was silent with the music up. Then, about five minutes later, Merriman turned down the music and said, "Things aren't so easy for you right now, huh?"

"I'd rather not really talk about it."

"Can I ask one question?" he asked.

"Sure."

"How's counseling?"

"It's okay," I said. "I used to think only really sick people were in counseling. But," I paused, "it's not like I thought it would be."

"I hear you. I was in counseling for two years after my parents divorced. That was a really tough time for me."

We got quiet again, but this time it was much more comfortable.

We arrived, went in, ordered and sat down after getting our drinks.

"So my sister's a Christian," I said to Merriman over my

mocha-latte.

"Yup," he said looking uncomfortable.

"What helped her get there?" I asked.

He looked at me, his blond eyebrows raised over his blue eyes but didn't answer.

"What did you say that mattered to her?"

His blond hair curled around his face from having been pressed down by his hat. "I don't really know," he said. "She asked questions and I answered them. It wasn't an easy decision for her to make." Then he added, "Mostly because of you."

I stared at him.

"Do you want to be where she is?" he asked in a whisper as he leaned forward.

I didn't want to think about it. My body wanted to fly out of my seat and tell him to shut up. Instead, I brought up the cup to my lips and hoped it wouldn't burn.

When Merriman didn't speak for a long time, I said, "It seems too hard." Then I added quickly, "Besides, I can't think about it right now. With my Bar Mitzvah and all."

"That's coming up soon, isn't it?" he asked.

"Two weeks."

He whistled. "What happens when it's over?"

"I become free," I replied. He studied me for a moment, and I changed the subject by saying, "Michelle, the field hockey captain, asked about you."

"What?" he said.

"Yeah, you know, Michelle, the one who dates Zeke occasionally."

"I know who you mean," he said. "Why was she asking about me?"

"Maybe she likes you or something."

Merriman shook his head. "I don't get it."

"What?" I asked.

"Michelle is not exactly deep, not exactly trustworthy."

"Maybe she sees something different in you."

Merriman smiled, "But my heart belongs to Grey."

That made me smile. "Then I'll let Michelle know she should comfort herself with Zeke."

Merriman grimaced. "I wouldn't wish that on my worst

enemy."

"Wouldn't that be Zeke?" I asked.

He thought for a second and said, "No, I think Zeke is more your enemy than mine. I have other enemies to contend with."

The coffee brewer started its high-pitched beeping and Van Morrison's "Moondance" played over the other people around us chatting.

"Are you going to teach Grey to snowboard?" I asked.

"We're running out of snow season and I think I'm going to be in Colorado next year."

"What?" I said my jaw dropping a little.

"Yeah, you know. I'm graduating and thinking about going to school in Colorado." He paused and said, "I was thinking about Gordon College, which is kind of close, but my sponsors have really pushed for me to move out there. I know I'm really close to the national level, so I could have a chance. We'll have to see."

"What about Grey?" I asked.

"I hope she'll join me out there when she graduates. But that's a year away."

"Doesn't that make you sad?" I asked.

Merriman paused and said, "You know, I'm just trying to not think about it and enjoy the time with her now."

I knew I was going to miss him.

***

Those two weeks flew by and before I could slow my world down, it was Friday, the day before my Bar Mitzvah. Poppy came into my room. Her long thick dark brown hair was braided down her back. She was wearing a long blue skirt and her Doc Marten boots.

My stomach had been in knots for a month. I could still eat a little, but food sat in me like pancakes on Saturday morning. I would belch the loudest belches. Mom could even hear me from the upstairs shower. She would come down all worried and ask if I was okay and eating enough. She even thought I should go the doctor's. It got so bad that one morning, with her hair wet and wearing a thin robe, I had to beg her to hang up the phone. At my last session, my counselor said I was fine and all this gas was normal.

When I farted, I could clear the room.

The schedule for the Bar Mitzvah weekend was packed.

Friday night: Mom and Dad lead services by lighting the candles and I lead in the singing over the bread and wine after the service was over. Didn't they know I couldn't sing?

Saturday morning: Stand in front of the congregation, my family, the other kids in my Hebrew school classes and look like a complete ass. Read out of the Torah and pray that I didn't throw up all over it. If you are killed for dropping it, what do they do if you upchuck on it?

Saturday afternoon: Attend a big party where Aunt Gaudy Lips would pinch my cheek and force me to dance with my fat cousin Rachel. Get called over by older men I don't know and have older women say, "I remember when you were only a baby. My, how you've grown up." And I have to smile and say, "Thank you," when in reality I would have no clue who these people were.

Saturday night: Count loot, sleep, thank God it was over. Also, sneak away and find Merriman. Thank him again for the Bible and ask him where to start reading.

"I don't want to do this," I groaned to Poppy as I flopped down on my unmade bed. The navy blue comforter was all in a heap with the flannel sheets. I was lying on the bump and it wasn't that comfortable.

"It will all be over tomorrow night," she said sitting down next to me.

"I can't wait," I replied.

"Just think. Tomorrow night, all of this nervousness will be gone."

"I'm not nervous," I lied. My stomach was bouncing around with such a violent fury that I thought Poppy could see it. It was like the monster in *Alien* was trying to rip itself out of my body.

When I told Bryce, my counselor, about it, he threw the basketball at the hoop and said, "Try to start breathing a lot more deeply at times when you think about all that you are facing. That will help you relax." He made the shot and passed the ball to me. I shot it and it went in. Bryce smiled at me, but he did not look surprised.

"Look," Poppy said, "try to remember that everyone out there doesn't know what you're saying. If you mess up, it's not that big a deal."

I grunted. "The only thing most people don't know is my Torah portion, which I have memorized. The rest *everyone* knows and if I mess that up, it will be obvious. Everyone will think I'm a dork."

"Nope," she smiled, "I don't know what's supposed to be said and what's not. So, you'll be perfect."

"Thanks."

I was still flopped on my bed. She stood up from where she was sitting, took my hand and started to pull me off the bed so I was standing up in front of her. Poppy put her arms around my waist and leaned her thin and confident body against mine. She put her head on my shoulder and my arms went around her waist and back. I lifted her braid as I wrapped my arms solidly around her. Poppy was warm and filling. I didn't want to let go, ever.

What if she thought I smelled, or that I wasn't hugging her right? Or that I wouldn't be good enough for her?

"Thank you," she whispered.

"For what?" I asked pulling away so I could look at her. Her eyes were deep pools and her cheeks were flushed.

"For being with me."

"For you, I would do almost anything." I meant it.

***

I was really quiet that Friday dinner. Well, I was always quiet at dinner. Mom looked over at me concerned a couple of times. "Are you okay?" she asked once.

I said, "Can someone please pass the asparagus?" It was passed and conversation continued as if Mom had said nothing. I hated asparagus.

"So tomorrow. Grey, what are your plans?" Dad asked.

"I'm getting my hair done at 7:45," she replied.

Mom said, "That's right. I'm taking you. You'll need to leave with me. My appointment is at 7:15. Maybe they can take you a little earlier. That would be nice."

"What time do we need to be at the synagogue?" Dad asked.

"The photographer is going to be there at 9:00. He wants to get shots of us before it starts. He's been to our synagogue before and knows the Rabbi doesn't like pictures being taken during the service."

"What about me?" I asked.

"You'll be fine. You'll get to the synagogue with all of us."

"What about my hair?"

"It looks great. You'll throw some gel in it and you will look fantastic," Mom said.

"I don't have any gel," I mumbled.

"Don't worry," Grey said. "You can use some of mine."

"Thanks," I said and pushed my meat around my plate.

"It will all be okay," Zeke said to me. "Mom remind him what I was like the night of mine."

Mom smiled a little at Zeke, "You stomped around the house saying you didn't look good enough, that your hair wasn't perfect and that everyone was going to notice your braces more than you."

"You'll see it's not such a big deal when it's all over," Zeke said to me and put more food in his mouth. I stayed silent.

Dinner was quiet for a couple of moments and then Grey cleared her throat and put her fork down. We all looked at her. "I know this is really bad timing, but I want you all to know something," she said, her voice soft and in a rush.

I looked up from my plate where I was taking my fork and smushing my asparagus up in between the tines. It would cut so that the white plate showed through the green strands of vegetable. I looked right at Grey for the first time all meal, she paled and spoke.

"I'm a Christian," she said.

Zeke stared. Dad almost choked and started to cough. Mom held her fork midair as she had been going down for more mashed yams. Dad put his fork down and tried to drink some water.

"I know. In a Jewish house, this is like a slap in the face. I need you to know I didn't take this decision lightly. I really thought about it. It has nothing to do with all of you. It has to do with my relationship with God."

"That's it," Dad said sitting up straight, now able to breathe. "How much more do you think this family can take?"

"It gets worse," Grey said.

"How?" Dad asked.

Mom had now put down her fork and was staring at her plate like she had never seen food before. Zeke was over his shock and was just looking at Grey with a facial expression I had never seen before; his eyebrows were raised and his lips were sucked in.

"Well," Grey said. "As you know, or maybe not because I've been real quiet about it.... I've been going to Merriman's church on Saturday and Sunday nights."

"My God," Dad said.

"Dad, listen," Grey said. "I'm not done yet. I realized that the Messiah we've been waiting for has come and many of the Jews just didn't see Jesus for who He was."

"Okay, stop right there," Dad was about to stand up.

"Wait, I haven't told you all of it yet."

"What?" Mom said in a whisper. "What is worse than this, Grey?"

"I've met with Merriman's Pastor...."

Dad groaned, slunked with his elbows on the table and his head in hands.

"...and I'm going to be baptized in three weeks at the Sunday morning service."

Mom stared at Grey. Dad still had his head in his hands. Zeke had a look of shock on his face and Grey looked at me. I winked back.

She smiled—quick and secret—at me and faced the rest of the family. They were silent. We waited.

At last, Dad said, "We're not talking about this now. It is *really* bad timing, Grey. It's Alex's Bar Mitzvah tomorrow."

"I know." Grey sighed and went back to playing with her food.

"I forbid you to see Merriman ever again," Mom blurted out.

"I think that may be unwise," Dad said. "It will only make Grey's attraction to him stronger."

After a pause, Dad added, "We do need to do something,

but we will deal with it after the Bar Mitzvah. Until then, nobody is to speak about this."

I, being helpful, tried to change the subject. "Since it is my birthday today. Is there a cake or anything?" Mom started to act like everything was fine and nothing weird was going on at all. "Right. Cake. Candles. Anyone want anything else to eat?"

Since no one spoke up, Grey got up to start clearing the dishes. Mom left her seat and went into the kitchen for the cake. They came out a couple of minutes later, when Grey was done clearing the table. My candles were dripping pink, yellow and blue wax on the chocolate icing of my cake and I blew them out.

I looked back and forth between Mom and Dad, who were still stunned, and pale. I began slicing. I made a mess by dropping the top half of the first piece on the tablecloth and getting chocolate everywhere.

Mom smiled at me. "You know-"

We looked at her. Her face had a faraway look, like she was looking at something that wasn't in the room, looking at something that only she could see.

"I just need to accept the fact that not everything turns out the way you expect it."

I continued to cut wedges of the cake while the rest of the table watched in silence.

***

Dad was at the front door and yelled for everyone to get in the car. I heard Grey run past my door to be first. I guessed that since she had been so displeasing at dinner she would try to be perfect the rest of the night. Mom began to yell for me to hurry up. She probably hollered three more times to get in the car, but I was still staring at myself in mirror when I heard the car horn honk. When I pulled the house door shut, Mom and Dad were both glaring at me through the front windshield.

Zeke was in the wayback of the minivan sitting with a small smile on his face and I took a seat next to Grey.

In the foyer of our synagogue, the Rabbi approached us. He shook Zeke's hand first and said, "I've been meaning to tell you,

Ezekiel, how much it has meant to have you working with the Hebrew school. I'm finding out that some of the boys are really beginning to look up to you. Maybe, when you're up to it, you will consider working with the youth group."

Zeke said, "Rabbi Cohn, I will certainly think about that. Thank you."

"You are doing a fine job," the Rabbi smiled.

The Rabbi approached Mom and Dad and said, "I know the circumstances under which Zeke has started to help, but I want you to know that I'm already seeing growth in him."

"Thank you," my father said as he shook the Rabbi's hand. "Good Sabbath to you."

Grey stood with her head down a little and she chewed on the side of her lip. I wanted to go over to her. To stand next to her. She had said and done what I couldn't. She had the strength to do what I was afraid of.

Shortly after the Rabbi walked away, my grandfather approached. He was once tall and strong. Now, he was little and hunched. He was with his sister, Aunt Rachel.

"There's the boy!" he said, his voice hoarse and kind of frail. "There's the Bar Mitzvah Boy! I'm so proud of you." He came and gave me a firm handshake. "Too old for hugs now. You're an adult!"

"Not until tomorrow," I said. His mention of hugs made me think of the hug with Poppy just hours ago, although it felt like ages now. The memory of it made my blood race and my pulse speed. Hugs were just getting good.

Aunt Rachel came up and kissed me on the cheek. "It's been so nice having your grandfather stay with me. With all the hubbub at your house, it's a shame he couldn't stay there like he usually does. I was pleased to be able to give him a traditional Jewish meal tonight, with noodle kugel."

"You know, you make the best noodle kugel," I replied.

She grinned at me, "When you get married, I'll give your wife my recipe."

"Thanks," I said, feeling a little sheepish. I knew it was mean, but I didn't think Aunt Rachel would live to see my wife. How could she? She was 72.

The Rabbi returned from his office and said to our group,

"It's time for you to get to the front of the sanctuary and sit down." We all started in procession.

"Alex," he called after me.

"Yes, Rabbi?" I asked turning back, my stomach dropping. What if he asked about my faith? What if he asked about my sister's? What if he wanted me to list off the 10 commandments. 1. Thou shalt love the Lord your God with all your heart, mind, soul and strength. 2. Thou shalt love your neighbor as yourself. 3. Thou shalt not commit adultery.....Something about coveting....Something about stealing....

"You okay?" he asked.

I stared at him.

"All set for tomorrow?"

"I think so."

"My wife has been telling me about your progress. You're going to be just fine."

"Thanks," I replied, still sweaty and shaken. *Don't ask if I love God, or Judaism. Don't ask if I know who I am....*

"Go ahead. Meet up with the rest of your family." He smiled and took my shoulder with a little shake, "Relax. You'll be great."

Quaking under his giant bear paw I scurried away to the sanctuary.

Once seated in between Mom and Dad, Mom took my hand and squeezed it. "Breathe," she said. "You don't have to do much tonight. Enjoy this."

The cantor came up to the front of the sanctuary and stood on the bema, the raised platform in the front. The cantor was the one who led in the singing during the services. She had short brown hair and a long black dress, with a mauve scarf, which matched the light flecks in the blue carpet that lined the sanctuary. Soon after, the Rabbi joined her and started the Friday evening service.

"Shabbat Shalom and good evening, everyone. Will you please rise for the singing of the Shema?" the Rabbi said opening the service.

Mom and Dad lit the Sabbath candles along the wall on the right side of the bema. They also had to say a blessing over the candles before and as they lit them.

There was a lot of standing and sitting. Some of the Roman Catholics at school called it church calisthenics. I didn't always remember when I was supposed to bow and bob in this one song. I would normally lift my head a little to look at the people in front to guide me. But I was in the front and the Rabbi was so far away and I was just supposed to know when to do the bowing, bobbing and leaning.

I tried to pay attention to Grey as all this was going on. She was sitting too far down the row to really see. She was going through the motions, I was sure. How could she not, sitting in the front? I also wanted to know how she was feeling. I mean, she didn't believe in this stuff anymore. I really wanted to ask her more, but I knew that I couldn't, or shouldn't. . . .

The service, like all services, was long. Sit, stand, sit, stand, bow, stand, sit. Responsively read all that's in the prayer book in italics and break out into song every five minutes. They always close the service by remembering the ones who have been lost; Grandmom was mentioned as were Dad's parents, Bubbie and Zay-dah. Mom always got teary eyed when the Rabbi read their names.

It was over by 9:30 p.m. We were sent to the back of the sanctuary, where there were three tables set up in a "U". The tables were covered with eclairs, Pepperidge Farm cookies and those cookies half dipped in chocolate and then covered in nonparailles and sprinkles. There were little cakes and brownies. In the center of the "U" was a loaf of challah and wine that needed to be blessed. We also sang a big long song that was all in Hebrew, and didn't make sense. I often got lost in the middle of it and had to stop and hum while everyone else around me sang. The worst part was, my whole family had to be up in the center of the "U" leading the congregation. I hated being up there. Everyone was facing me. I had to look everywhere I could but out at the crowd to keep myself sane. I wound up staring at a spot on the floor and wished that the wood would splinter and crack, grab my shoelace and pull me into its gaping hole. Then the wood would come back together and appear as it had before it gorged itself on me.

When I was set free, I attacked the cookies with sprinkles. Then I went over to the punch bowl, which had fruit punch and rainbow sherbet in it. I didn't really want any, but took some anyway. My stomach began to clench the second I swallowed three sips.

A kid in Hebrew School with me, Andrew, came up. He was wearing khaki pants, a white shirt and a green tie with Alfred E. Newman from Mad Magazine on it. Andrew asked, "What's up?"

"Nothing."

"I go next week," he said.

"Right."

"Nervous?" he asked.

"I'm all right. It's not that bad. Besides, tomorrow there's the party and I'm going to be able to eat anything I want." But I was lying. I looked forward to the party being over. The party wasn't really for me; Mom and Dad made the invitation list and it was mostly their friends and family who were coming.

"Who did you invite?" Andrew asked.

"A whole bunch of family members; I don't know."

"Me too," Andrew said. "Mom made up the list and I'll barely have any friends there."

I started to look around the room for Grey. She was the only one who I even wanted to be near.

I scanned past old people, my grandfather and Aunt Rachel among them. I also scanned past the kids I go to Hebrew school with running up to the Rabbi to take slips of paper from him to prove that they had been to the service. My eyes caught the movement of someone bringing their arm up and swooping it through their hair. I brought my eyes to focus on the back corner of the room where a guy was talking to Grey. I couldn't see who he was, but I could see the flurry of her hands in her hair. A dead give-away that she wasn't okay.

Andrew was still standing next to me, but watching Grey, I had forgotten about him.

Finally, he said, "I'm going to go see if I can find my mom and get out of here."

"Wish I could do that," I said not looking at him. My eyes were glued to the way the guy had Grey in the corner.

"Good luck tomorrow," Andrew replied over his shoulder as he slumped into the crowd.

I stood and stared until Dad came up asking if I was ready to head out.

"I know it's early, but you have a big day tomorrow." Then he surprised me by saying, "Did you know about Grey?"

"Yes."

"Why didn't you tell us?"

"I'm not a rat."

"But she has you questioning?"

I didn't say anything.

"Do you know where she is?" Dad asked.

"Over there," I said pointing to the corner where she was still playing with her hair and talking to that guy.

"Ah, Jacob Majorwitz caught up with her," he said. "He's a nice boy."

"She's dating Merriman," I replied.

"One can hope," Dad sighed and clapped me on the shoulder. "Let's get you home to bed."

Dad caught Mom's eye. She was talking to Grey's tutor from when Grey was working on her Bat Mitzvah. Mom moved toward Grey. Grey, seeing her coming, made a little wave at Mom and shortly afterward joined the rest of us in the main foyer.

"Where's Zeke?" Dad asked looking around.

"He was in the kitchen helping clean up. He said he would meet us at the car," Mom replied.

Dad smiled and said, "That's really nice to hear."

We all went out and piled into the van. Zeke joined us about five minutes later.

Grey and I sat next to each other in the seat all the way in the back.

"Who were you talking to?" I whispered.

"Some guy I went to Hebrew school with."

We were quiet as Dad pulled out of the synagogue's driveway. About five minutes down the road, Grey whispered to me, "I didn't know what to say to him. He invited me to go to youth group at the synagogue. I told him that I was going to youth group at Merriman's church; he didn't seem impressed."

"So, how was the service?"

"Same as always," she said. "No feeling, nothing like it is at church. . . . It's like we pray in synagogue and the prayers bounce off the ceiling back down to us. Like they don't get to God."

"I know what you mean," I whispered back.

We both got quiet.

I let my mind think of other things, like Poppy and how much I wished she were here.

***

Once back at home, there was a voice mail message from Poppy and Merriman. It was too late to call Poppy back, so Grey got to use the phone for a while. Mom and Dad made decaffeinated tea in the kitchen, then moved to their study to talk. I was afraid of what they were saying.

Up in my room, I pulled on my blue and gray plaid pajama pants and flicked off the switch on the wall next to the door, turning off the overhead light. The moon was bright outside and left a pale square of light on my gray-blue carpet. I felt my way in the semi-dark, flopped on my bed, leaned over and turned on the table lamp on the nightstand. My prayer book was lying next to the lamp; I pulled it onto my lap. I flipped it open to the worn, brown photocopy of my Torah portion one more time before I went to bed. I opened it up and looked at it, but my eyes didn't want to focus. The digital clock on the little nighttable read in red numbers, 10:41.

Tomorrow, I would stand in front of everyone, friends and family, Poppy and Zeke to "read" a whole bunch of weird squiggles on a page in a heavy scroll. I would give a speech I knew was cheesy. I was expected to go to sleep tonight?

I leaned over and turned out the light. I slumped down on my bed, got under the covers and rolled to one side. I stared at the black behind my eyelids. I opened my mouth and started to drool in the hope that would help me fall asleep.

I might have dozed off.

I heard Dad open the door and whisper, "You awake, slugger?"

"UMMMmmmmm," came out of my mouth. But, in my mind, I had heard myself say, "Yup."

"Can I talk to you?"

"Sure," I tried to say as I sat up.

"I know it's late and you have a big day tomorrow. I just wanted to let you know how proud your mother and I are of you."

I looked at him. He was a silhouette in the light from the hall as it shone in a narrow rectangle of the open doorway. The square of moonlight was brighter on the carpet.

Dad came over to my bed. I moved my legs out of the way for him; he didn't sit down as I had expected him to.

Instead, he tousled my hair and said, "You should go to sleep. Big day tomorrow."

"Goodnight," I said.

"Love you, Sport," he replied.

"Love you too," I mumbled as my eyes closed and I started to dream.

***

I awoke with a start and sat bolt upright in bed. My heart was pounding and I could hear the ga-thumps in my ears. There was bright sunlight pouring in my room. What if I had slept late? What if it was all over and I had missed it?

I heard the sound of many voices downstairs in the kitchen. Mom yelled up the steps. "Grey! Get up and out of bed! We need to be there in 10 minutes!"

Be where? Where were they going? Didn't I need to be there too? I jumped out of bed and flung myself out my bedroom door. Grey was tripping down the hall past me in a little pink tank top and pink, red and white plaid pants, not too unlike the blue and gray ones I was wearing. She gave me a feeble wave and a good morning as she lead the way downstairs to the kitchen.

Everyone, except Zeke, was now congregated around the breakfast bar eating and drinking coffee. Grandfather and Aunt Rachel were there as well. They were both dressed up. Grandfather had on a navy blue suit and a maroon tie with swirling Hebrew letters in gray and blue and gold. Aunt Rachel was in a long flowy purple shirt and a navy blue flowy skirt with lots of bright flowers all over it. She had a hot pink scarf tied around her neck. I shook my head at its brightness and how it affected my brain.

They were both at the kitchen table eating oatmeal.

Mom, the second she saw Grey, started to rail. "Get your butt back upstairs and shower. Not a long one either. We need to leave *now*. Go! Don't worry about getting your hair wet, they will take care of it there."

Grey, now with a cup of coffee in her hand, went back up the stairs without even saying, "Good morning," to anyone. Soon we heard the sound of water running through the pipes.

"That girl needs to use her alarm. I told her last night at dinner what time I wanted to leave. I can't believe—" and what Mom couldn't believe I didn't hear because she left the room still mumbling to herself.

"What time is it?" I panicked looking around.

"Relax, you have two hours before we have to leave," Dad said handing me a Boston Creme doughnut, my favorite.

"Then why am I awake?" I asked.

"That was your choice."

I started to gobble the doughnut so that the cream didn't drip everywhere.

Mom came back in the room. "Alex, go upstairs and start getting ready. I want you done early then maybe Grey or your father can get you over to the synagogue so that you can get settled and the photographer can maybe get a start on you before everyone else gets there."

I stood there trying to understand what she had just said, wiping chocolate off my hands with a used napkin lying on the counter in front of me.

"Move!" she yelled and I jumped. I started to turn and run. Instead, I plowed into Grey, who was standing behind me in a white plush towel.

Grey jumped, screamed and gripped the top of the towel hooked just above her chest. "Really, Alex!" she yelled almost falling over. I grabbed one of her elbows and Dad was there in seconds behind her so that she only got knocked into his shoulder.

"That was my fault," Mom laughed. "You can't go to the

beauty parlor like that Grey! What are you doing?"

"I want the clothes I washed last night," she said. "I'll be ready in two seconds." She left the room to go to the laundry room and more like one minute later she was wearing jeans and a baggy green zipper sweatshirt that said, "Gordon College" on it.

"Where did you get that?" Mom asked.

"Merriman," she said.

Mom rolled her eyes, grabbed her purse and said, "Let's get out of here."

Grey followed her out the door.

I went upstairs and took the longest shower I had in a week, a full half hour. I allowed the water to wash down my body and pool around my toes. I stared into the showerhead, spraying water down on me and tried to erase my mind. It was racing through all of the moments of the day that lay ahead. I said out loud into the streaming water, "Shabbat Shalom, everybody. Please rise for the Shema." They weren't even my lines; they were the Rabbi's.

I was still standing in my towel in the open bathroom when Grey and Mom returned. Grey stuck her head in.

"What do you think of my hair?" she asked.

"Looks great," I said as I studied her hair which had been twisted and wrapped into a crazy bun on the back of her head. She had a wisp or two curling around the sides of her face.

She looked at me and said, "Here," as she threw a little white round container at me.

As I reached out to catch it, I was afraid the towel I was wearing would slip, fall off and reveal my rodents to my sister.

"What's this?" I asked placing the container on the sink so that I could tighten my towel.

"Molding Mud," she said with a grin.

"What?" I asked taking the container and opened the lid to reveal this gross creamy-yellow substance.

"Take a little into your palm and rub both palms together fast until they get hot. Then, rub it all through your hair."

"You want me to put this in my hair?" I asked dumbstruck.

"It will look fantastic. Trust me."

I put the white plastic container up to my nose. It smelled sweet like the stuff you lick on envelopes.

***

I went into my room with a slick, curl-spiked 'do enhanced by the Molding Mud. Over at my dresser, I pulled out my coolest boxers, Joe Boxers with yellow smiley faces. I took the new clothes off their hangers and slid the shirt up my arms and onto my back. I stared at its rich blue as I buttoned the white buttons. I also made sure the that khaki pants didn't show the smiley faces through the material. I was all good. I was even cooler than I was in the store. The shimmery tie sparkled against the navy blue shirt.

When I went downstairs, Dad, having never seen the clothes on, whistled. Grey, still in her jeans and sweatshirt, was shoving Cheerios in her mouth as she stood by the sink. Her jaw fell and her spoon lay lifeless in the bowl with her hand still on the handle. "Wow," she whispered.

I felt the heat rush up into my cheeks. "Thanks."

"Let's get out of here soon before Mom comes back and whisks us out the door. That will mess both of us up," she said indicating her hair. I realized that she was wearing a little bit of dark blue eyeshadow and a touch of blush. I looked at her and the way she moved. Grey never wears make-up and it made her seem a lot older than just a junior.

Dad was in a dark suit with a white shirt underneath and a navy blue tie.

"Looks like we're all in the navy theme," Grey said. "Just wait until you see what I'm wearing."

"Did you go with Merriman to pick it out?" I asked.

"Yup," she said.

"Then you will look fantastic," I said.

"Give me ten minutes and then we'll be off," she said as she charged up the stairs.

***

Rabbi came into the synagogue's foyer where I was standing, then left. I needed to get a yarmulka, the beanie-like hat that all men have to wear. You can't go into the sanctuary without one. Did I wear one last night? Don't remember. Maybe. Maybe it was navy and didn't sit on my head right. Maybe it gave me a cone-head. Today, got to find the right one. White, look for the white cotton, not satin, ones that have silver along the edges. The satin ones never sit right. Dig. Dig. Dig. Rummage. Maroon. Navy Blue. Powder Blue. Pink. Bright orange. Who would have orange? I looked at the inside and printed in green it said, "On the occasion of Jacob Majorwitz becoming a Bar Mitzvah on Saturday, October 31st." Jacob Majorwitz, who was he? I recognized the name. . . . Of course, that guy talking to Grey last night. How appropriate.

"Ready?" Rabbi asked as he walked by.

I shook my head no but said, "Yes."

He chuckled and said, "Remember you are not alone. Everyone goes through this. Your brother did, your sister did, the guy last week did and the guy next week will."

Pictures. Up at the bema. My parents wanted the scroll out and open so we could fake a reading. Rabbi came. He took one out. Undressed it. Unrolled it. Photos. Red spots in front of my eyes that glowed sea-green and teal and orange everywhere I looked for the next 25 minutes.

"You look great!" "Oh, what a fabulous tie!" "Where did you get that outfit?" "Man! I wish I could get my son to wear these kinds of clothes."

Smile. Smile. Stomach churning and crawling. Swallow. Smile. Swallow. Grin. Oh, another picture. Spots.

"How is the Bar Mitzvah boy?" Oh, I should remember her name. "We're so proud of you," she kissed my cheek. They all kissed my cheek. Kissed and left lipstick that they then tried to rub off leaving a red mark. I would have a permanent red, orange and pink mark on both cheeks by the end of the day and it would show up in all the pictures. I went to Mom and had her take a tissue to my face. She had lots of tissues.

Bema. Sat in leather chair that exhaled as I sunk into it. I needed to face the congregation and look attentive. I needed to breathe.

People were coming in. Rabbi was sitting next to me. Aunt Gaudy-lips with big-haired Rachel walked in. They were in matching mauve V-neck sweaters and the same tight black skirts.

They even did their make-up the same, mauve eye shadow and thick, slimy gloss on their lips. I rolled my eyes and looked to the Rabbi to see if he noticed them. I wonder if he went home and reported what he saw. Who had the biggest hair, the biggest rings, the biggest noses.

Tick, Tick. I looked at my watch. Almost 10:00. We start at 10:00. Can't they see I'm in agony?

The Rabbi stood. Mom noticed. She started to walk to the front. Dad followed. Grey didn't notice, she was taking grandfather to his seat. Zeke came up to the front and sat at the end of the chairs on the bema. The Rabbi greeted Zeke; they stood talking and smiling at each other.

"Shabbat Shalom and good morning everybody," the Rabbi said into the microphone. My stomach leapt and the singing started. I would have sung, but the thought of puke all over the front of the sanctuary stopped me. Dad was standing next to me. Mom next to him, Grey and then Zeke. I looked over at Dad. He winked at me. I opened my mouth, closed it and swallowed and then opened it again and sang.

It all happened so fast after that. Sat and stood. Sang and recited. I got to the microphone and asked the congregation to join me in the prayer book on page 320 and it was a blur.

The Torah came out. We sang and walked it around the congregation. People kissed their prayer books or prayer shawls and touched the Torah with them as it came around. The Rabbi undressed the white paper with thin stitching that held it together. He unscrolled it. The letters were brown. They were done by hand, as was the stitching. If no one was supposed to touch the Torah directly, how could it be all be done by hand?

I used the pointer and read the words that I knew in my head so well I didn't need to read them. My stomach was calmer by this point. I didn't look out to the congregation and I spoke fast. "Get it done. Get it done. *Slow down*. Get it done," played over and over in the back of my mind. I knew I had the tendency to plow ahead fast. When I was very uncomfortable, I plowed even faster. My hand was hot on the silver pointer and the Rabbi had to help me guide it because my hand was so shaky that I probably would have lost the line I was on.

We redressed the Torah and put it back in its home, the ark.

Dad smiled and Mom kissed my cheek as they sat down to listen to my speech. I stood in front of the congregation and for the first time was brave enough to allow my eyes to scan who was there. Aunt Gaudy-lips was next to Aunt Rachel and Grandfather. I moved my eyes back and I saw Poppy. She was with her parents. She was leaning forward. She was wearing a light pink sweater. She smiled and blushed, looking down. I looked down at the papers in front of me and began to read my speech:

"I was excited about my Torah portion being about the kosher laws because of how important food is to me. (A few people chuckled.) But kosher laws are more than just about food, they are about God's love for us. As I stand here before you, the world is a mess. People do awful things to each other everywhere. (I glanced to Zeke, and he was looking right at me.) Not just on a big scale, like the World Trade Towers or the Holocaust, but on a littler scale, like torment done in school hallways or siblings who make the lives of their brothers or sisters miserable. Looking at these things, the kosher laws may not seem important. Why would God care if we ate pig or a lobster?

It goes deeper than what you put in your mouth. It's about the realization that we are not alone on this planet. We need to be focused on God. I heard someone on the radio one morning as I was waking up say that the United States has invited God out of their society and like a gentleman, He has left. If we started honoring Him more, perhaps things would begin to make more sense...."

When I was done, the Rabbi stood and spoke to me at the podium. He said, "Alex, you've really struggled with the work it takes to become a Bar Mitzvah. You rose to the challenge and have showed all of us that you can do a job we can all be proud of. You've shown yourself to be willful, but also very caring and sensitive. You have an active curiosity about your religion and I encourage you to pursue that here at the synagogue in the years to come."

"You have passions, Alex. Don't hide from them, pursue

them and become the man that we all see inside your boy shape. You are destined for greatness, push on and meet the challenges ahead of you, in the same way that you faced the challenges of becoming a Bar Mitzvah."

I blushed. I hated being up in front of everyone being told nice things about me. Insult me, tell me I'm stupid and useless. I would understand that a lot more than these nice words. I wanted to run. But, I also wanted to swallow the words the Rabbi was saying and never forget them. It sounded like he knew me, or that he had kept in touch with my progress of becoming a Bar Mitzvah. My face paled at the thought that he knew about the questions I had been asking his wife. I mean, how could he not know? What was I thinking? I wanted to hit myself on the forehead, but I forced myself to breathe. The oxygen entering my lungs made me a little light-headed and dizzy. I put my hand on the podium to steady myself. He gave me a bunch of books, which I grabbed in obvious greed. Then it was all over. He was saying the mourner's kaddish and listing names. Mom was crying, again.

"Shabbat Shalom, good shabbish everyone."

***

It was all a fog from there. We left the synagogue and headed over to the place Mom booked for the reception, Harrington House. The walls were cream and the curtains forest green. The tablecloths were all navy blue. There was a circular wooden dance floor in the front of the room where the DJ had set up his heavy black equipment. Everywhere but where the dance floor was, there was a dark green carpet to match the curtains.

The servers, all in tuxedos and black bow-ties, welcomed the guests with hors d'oeuvres while I had to get pictures taken with every member of my family. At one point the tray with tiny hot dogs wrapped in croissant bread went by. "That's not kosher," I said pointing.

Mom tutted and said, "Hush your mouth. Your brother loves them."

When I thought about the pictures, I didn't mind them much because they kept me away from all of the smooching aunts and their hideous lipstick. But then, my eyes caught sight of Poppy's long red wool coat that she only wears on special occasions. Her cheeks were flushed and she was standing with her parents. They were talking, but she glanced over at me, smiled and waved. I smiled to her and the photographer said, "Great, Alex! Well done. Keep that up." My smile faded almost immediately and the photographer decided to end the photo session early.

Poppy was the only friend who could attend. I only invited Poppy and Matters, but Matters had to go to his grandmother's for the weekend. He had offered to invite Michelle the Cheetah in his place.

"That's okay," I had said to him. "It might make Zeke more happy than he deserves to be."

Poppy and I got to sit next to each other, with Grey, Zeke and Merriman, whom I begged my Mom and Dad to invite. But today, they were straining to be nice to him at all. Come to think of it, they really weren't talking to Grey either. They sort of told her she looked nice and let the other relatives ask her questions about sports, or other interests she had.

Also at my table was my cousin, Rachel - Gaudy-lips' daughter, who was named for her living grandmother (which was not an okay thing), and two other cousins I didn't really know named, Joshua and Rebecca. The DJ played music Mom really loved, including Barbara Striesand. Who listens to Barbara Striesand? Then the DJ called all of the kids out onto the floor and we had a hoola-hoop contest. Who thought up this stuff?

Who would have thought that my cousin Rachel was so good with a hoola-hoop? She looked over at Poppy and smirked, "It must be all of the gymnastics lessons."

Poppy was so smooth. She said, "Yeah, painting in oils doesn't make you graceful. It just gets you lots of money in contests."

Rachel frowned at her and said, "What contests have you ever won?"

Poppy smiled, "Oh, you probably wouldn't have ever seen any of them. They're all really high profile and only the really sophisticated magazines ever print my work."

I was trying really hard to look serious and not grin like mad at Poppy's wild stories.

"Yeah, well, I'm the first place holder for the floor routine in my division," Rachel said all important and proud.

"Oh, that's great," Poppy said. "Did Alex tell you that the Boston's Museum of Fine Arts curator called me to see if he could do a small showing of my work?"

Rachel looked at me, her mouth open and her eyes unable to blink.

"Oh," I said. "I forgot. I mean with the Bar Mitzvah and all, a lot has been on my mind."

"That's understandable," said Poppy. "Especially since I don't care about it anyway. My mom makes such a big deal of it, but she's promised me that she won't talk about it at all today. It is Alex's day."

Rachel huffed off a few minutes later. Then, Poppy grabbed my hand and squeezed it. "That was so fun."

I held her hand tight in mine. I looked at her. Our eyes met. I didn't care who saw and the photographer came by at that moment and snapped a picture. Both Poppy and I blushed big time.

Grey and Merriman danced together every song they could. Both slow and fast, but I noticed they were only on the floor when they could blend in with other people. It was time to eat; we had Chicken Kiev, which I was a little disappointed to admit, wasn't kosher; Mom and Dad were breaking Jewish laws everywhere.

As the party began to wrap up at four o'clock, there were gifts piled about four feet high on the table by the entrance. There was a basket for cards that was overflowing. I eyed both in flat-out greed while Poppy's parents arranged for her to come back to my house

When it was over, I didn't feel any different. I was the same old Alex, only really tired.

***

Poppy watched me open gifts and tally up the checks. The money amount was outrageous, in the thousands. Mom and Dad decided to talk to a financial planner.

The party was okay. I didn't really like the DJ. Mom picked

him; she loved him. Not that there was much he could do, there weren't many kids there. I knew everyone there. I just hated how wherever I went, people wanted to stop me and talk.

It was a cool way to get an insane amount of stuff though. Merriman gave me a CD he mixed.

***

As we all stood around in the kitchen drinking Cokes and chatting, I turned to Merriman and said, "What did you think of today?"

"I didn't understand it all, but it sounded cool."

I said, "I know what you mean."

"Hey," Merriman said, "I know that the CD doesn't seem like much. But, trust me. It's important."

I laughed. "I'll keep that in mind before I completely diss the whole thing."

I excused myself from them, Poppy, Grey, Merriman, so I could pull on an old purple sweatshirt, with holes at the bottom of the sleeves that I could put my thumbs through, and my pajama bottoms. Though I loved the khakis and tie and had gotten many compliments on them, I was really glad to change.

When I came back down, Poppy, Grey and Merriman were all in jeans and bulky sweaters or sweatshirts (Grey in the Gordon College one). Grandfather and Aunt Rachel still looked quite content in their fancy clothes. Mom had broken out some leftovers including my Bar Mitzvah cake.

Mom tousled my hair and said, "You done good."

Dad agreed, raising his fork saying, "Hear, Hear!"

Zeke was shoveling cake into his mouth. Grey and Merriman went for a walk. Mom and Dad frowned after them as they left. Poppy and I hung out watching T.V., my brain couldn't do more than that. It took all I had to stay awake. But the heat of her hand was all there was in the world. That was when Poppy leaned over, closed her eyes and pressed her warm lips to my cheek. It was indescribable and I was left staring at her, speechless. She smiled sweetly and curled up in a ball with her head on my chest. I brought my hand up and played with her hair until her father came to take her home.

Her father shook my hand when I walked Poppy to the door. "Congratulations," he said. Poppy blushed and they left.

I said goodnight to everyone, even though it was only ten o'clock. I slunk up the stairs, too tired to move any faster.

***

Alone in my room with only the night table lamp on, I moved on tiptoe to the shut closet door. The door had been staring at me for days and every time I came into my bedroom, I had to get out fast for fear that it would suck me toward it and never let me go. But I wasn't afraid of my closet. It was my blanket, Yaba.

Mom said Yaba had once been white. Now, Yaba was cream with faded light green elephants and pale purple lions. When I was seven, Zeke punched me for the first time. It was because I was sitting on Yaba. Yaba was there and forgiving when I was sick and threw up all over him. He understood my tears the time that Grey fell out of the tree she was climbing and cut her mouth open and had to be rushed to the hospital. Yaba had been waiting for me, quiet and soft in his bulky folds, when I came home from the first day of kindergarten scared and shaken.

Now, Yaba was hiding in the back corner of my closet in a wadded up ball next to the games like Monopoly, Backgammon, and Battleship, all in a neat stack.

I squeaked the closet door open. My exhausted calf muscles strained to stand on tiptoes, heat rushing up and down my legs. I reached my hand up to the back. Only the top part of my middle finger touched Yaba where he was crouching. I wanted to whisper, "Come on." Instead, I jumped, and tugged. As I landed, Yaba fell off the shelf, where my hands were waiting to catch him.

I turned to the side, checking the door to my room, making sure I was really alone. Unfolding the ball Yaba was tucked into, I revealed the hard covered Bible Merriman had given me. The Bible Grey had told me to hide months ago.

I moved to my bed and sat down on it. In one hand I still held the soft baby blanket, the other, the book. I lifted Yaba up to my face, his softness was home and smelled sweet.

I sat on my bed, my back against the wall. I dropped Yaba into my lap and brought the book down on top.

There were two different kinds of words on the pages. Big at the top, and smaller at the bottom in little footnotes. I flipped to the back, maps colored in pastels showing Israel during different periods.

As I was flipping through the thin pages, I heard Grey's footsteps going down the hall toward her bedroom.

I left Yaba on my bed, walked to my door, and peaked out into the hallway. The overhead light was on and the hall was empty. I shoved the cool book up my shirt and hugged it to my chest.

I tiptoed to Grey's door. I thought I heard her soft call of *come in* when I knocked. I wasn't sure. Still, I thought I heard something, so I cracked the door open and stuck my head in.

She was in her pajamas, in her bed. Reading. Reading the black leather-covered Bible that Merriman had given her months before, in the hallway at school.

Grey looked at me, paled under the harsh light of her bedside lamp.

"What's up, Alex?"   She already knew the answer but needed to hear me say it.

"Can we talk?"